DEAD ON THE WIND

"The dangerous, fascinating world of long distance, single handed yacht racing is full of remarkable characters and daring feats, making it an especially intriguing setting for a high-seas whodunit. Marlin Bree knows this arena well, and his well-crafted tale of mystery and adventure makes for gripping reading.
— Herb McCormick, **Cruising World**

"Marlin Bree's debut novel packs all the adventure of his award-winning fiction with enough twists and turns to keep you reading through the night. *Dead on the Wind* deserves a spot on every boater's reading list." —Yvonne Hill, **The Ensign**

BROKEN SEAS
TRUE TALES OF EXTRAORDINARY SEAFARING ADVENTURES

"It is no accident that our history books are filled with adventures of the sea. Sailors and non-sailors are captivated by nautical stories. Marlin Bree's new book, *Broken Seas,* explains in gripping detail tales from both the Great Lakes and the ocean. When reading this book you will feel like you are on board during some of the harshest calamities in recent history."
— Gary Jobson, World-class sailor and boating author

"Marlin Bree's new book *Broken Seas* will crank up your adrenaline and jump-start your pulse. Bree's prose puts you right in the middle of these extraordinary true adventures. From crossing the Pacific in a 10-footer to braving a November blow on Lake Superior, this book will leave you with spray on your face, wind in your hair and an insatiable itching to get out on the water. Don't miss it."
— Yvonne Hill, Editor of **The Ensign**

"Marlin Bree's first-hand knowledge of monster waves and survival has enabled him to vividly and accurately describe six true adventures in *Broken Seas*. This book details triumph and tragedy and is a must-read for sailors, and even landlubbers will enjoy these amazing tales."
— Chuck Luttrell, Author of **Heavy Weather Boating Emergencies**

"*Broken Seas* is a pleasure to read. The seafaring adventures are well researched, the characters and their struggles come to life."— Capt. Thom Burns, **Northern Breezes**

WAKE OF THE GREEN STORM
A SURVIVOR'S TALE

"...the monstrous storm system invaded the lake...and the largest, angriest waves he's ever experienced tore at his small craft. He was reasonably sure he'd not live to see the next day."
— Don Boxmeyer, **St. Paul Pioneer Press**

"A perilous tale" — **Minneapolis StarTribune**

"Now, here's some reading for a dark and stormy night, but only if you are safely tied to the dock. Marlin Bree's *Wake of the Green Storm* tells of his incredible voyage in a 20-foot, wooden sailboat across Lake Superior's north Shore. All this, a personal experience of Lake Superior legends by a man who, by chasing them, became a legend himself. —**Great Lakes Cruiser**

"...can equal any oceanic adventure." — **San Diego Log**

IN THE TEETH OF THE NORTHEASTER
A SOLO VOYAGE ON LAKE SUPERIOR

"Will set your teeth on edge."— **Rocky Mountain News**

"An adventure — he encountered several fierce storms – and an anecdotal history of the lake with tidbits on Indians, voyageurs, miners, sea captains ... as well as tales of wind, weather icy (and sometimes frozen) water, and shipwrecks. — **Booklist**

"Bree and his Persistence dared greatly, struggled greatly, and had a worthy run, told with touching candor. Bree is at his best when the lake was at its worst." — **Wilmington Evening Journal**

"A voyageur's tale of sailing solo, occasionally in dangerous dark seas on Lake Superior. A lovingly written story."
— **Baltimore Sun**

"Captures once again the feel and wild spirit of one of the most beautiful but treacherous bodies of water in the world."
—**Minneapolis StarTribune**

MARITIME BOOKS
BY
MARLIN BREE

BROKEN SEAS
True tales of extraordinary seafaring adventures

WAKE
OF THE
GREEN STORM
A Survivor's Tale

IN THE TEETH
OF THE
NORTHEASTER
A Solo Voyage on Lake Superior

CALL
OF THE
NORTH WIND
Voyages and Adventures on Lake Superior

BOAT LOG
& RECORD
The perfect small craft record keeper
for cruises, expenses and maintenance

ALSO

BY GERRY SPIESS
WITH MARLIN BREE

ALONE
AGAINST
THE
ATLANTIC

DEAD
ON THE
WIND

A NOVEL BY

MARLIN BREE

Marlor Press
Saint Paul, MN

Handwritten inscription:
For Kim
A fellow
Superior
sailor.
—[signature]
3-26-2015

DEAD
ON THE
WIND

Copyright 2015
By MARLIN BREE

Published by Marlor Press, Inc.
Cover Design by Theresa Gedig/ DigDesign

ISBN 978-1-892147-31-8

EPUB 978-1-892147-33-2

Manufactured in the United States of America

Distributed to the book trade in the USA
By Independent Publishers Group, Chicago

First Edition

MARLOR PRESS, INC.

4304 Brigadoon Drive
Saint Paul, MN 55126

FOR

LORIS

'Till we
meet again
on that
far distant
shore

Beyond 40 degrees south,
there is no law.
Below 50,
there is no god.

THE

TASMAN SEA

PROLOGUE

JOLLY SWAGWOMAN caught the storm's initial gusts and
heeled over. Spray flashing from its bow, the big sloop dug its
shoulder in, careening between dark troughs and picking up speed
all the way.

Marci Whitman braced herself against the thrumming wheel,
feet spread wide apart, watching as the knotmeter's red numbers
flashed ever higher: 18...19 ...touching 20 knots.

The boat began to vibrate and shake, the twin rudders' high-
speed hum became a scream. From behind the great machine, a
rooster tail of water shot skyward.

The bow slashed into a wave, cutting deep. A water torrent
surged back, slapping Marci in the face.

"You beauty!" she yelled, adrenaline surging.

Jolly Swagwoman was alive in her hands, surging through the
sea with vitality. Its sails, hull and rudder all had messages for
her. The boat told her what it felt and what it wanted to do.

She was its keeper — and lover. As long as she understood, she
would be safe.

A reef in the mainsail? No, not yet. There was much to learn
about the big boat. It was handling well and she had to know its
secrets. Moreover, she had to have faith—implicit faith in her
boat—where they were going.

Today was proving day for her and the giant craft—out in blue
water on its first independent sea trials. She had rated a salute
from the Royal Yacht Club in Sydney as she sailed alone out from
the harbor. Just her and her boat; no following crew in a Zodiac.
None of the usual helpers on board, either. She loved it.

On the wharves of the Sydney Opera House, thousands of fans
cheered and waved flags. She was their champion, their "Golden
Girl." Her nickname was "Gee Gee."

Her boat was created on the Sydney waterfront, built and

equipped there, and designed to conquer the boisterous waters of the world. It employed the latest maritime technologies including carbon fibre and composites.

Marci's boat was equipped with a special, large diameter steering wheel custom made of carbon fiber. That made it very light, easy to spin, and gave her a good feel for what the twin giant rudders sticking deep below her were doing. She needed speed and speed came with smoothness.

She stood erectly behind the giant wheel, glancing up at the towering mast, bending slightly at the masthead, and briefly studied the set of the mainsail. Sails bar taut. Good airflow. All powered up. *We're flying.*

To see over the wheel, so she did not have to stand on her tip toes, she had her father build a raised platform. This worked well. Beneath her sea boots, she could feel the bite of the twin carbon fiber rudders, both digging in and keeping her roaring beast on track.

An autopilot could take over some of the steering chores, but in heavy going, hand steering was hands-down the best for speed. Marci planned to spend a lot of time at the wheel, mindful that when you were slashing through big waves, you needed a live body at the wheel.

Races were won by those who got the least sleep and who helmed the most. Racing big boats was not a thing you learned in advance, but something you had to get out there and do.

Now in 1992, this was the Golden Age of giant sailboats racing around the world in sometimes dark and dangerous seas. Superb sailboat technology and advanced construction techniques and materials were winning over the waves and the storms.

But nothing prepared her for the raw power of the big boat. Sailboats are alive in a way no other boat is, ever,

"*You go, girl!*" She patted the thrumming wheel.

She would be the only female sailor out there, so she'd have to grind it out with the big boys. Racers. No quarter given. This was what she had trained to do. She was up for it.

It would be an adrenaline rush—a monumental wind-mad high.

*   *   *

The bow stuck itself in a wave and scooped up green water as well as bunches of foam, hurling it back to Marci.

It was a slap in the face. Cold. Even dressed in her heavy duty foulies, her head protected in her hood and her eyes shaded by a baseball cap, she barely ducked the onslaught.

She inhaled sharply, then adjusted her amber-tinted goggles and wisped a stray strand of damp blond hair off her forehead.

She swore, then grinned. The fun meter was definitely in the red.

* * *

It was time. She gritted her teeth as she swung the wheel hard over to begin her last point of sail. This would be a tight reach, with the breeze just forward of the beam, the fastest run —and the hardest on the boat.

A chill wave of instinct sweep over her. She had to do this.

"Fear is not important," she chanted to herself. "It's what you do with it. To win you've got to try. And keep on trying until you do win."

Jolly Swagwoman heeled precipitously as it lunged and jumped through the waves.

Marci could feel the boat straining and creaking beneath her as every sail, every line, every winch loaded up at maximum pressure. Then it seemed to take off.

...22 knots, the knotmeter glowed. *Swagwoman* was planing like a powerboat.

"Fantastic!" Marci yelled, her faith in her great machine justified.

The big boat was working hard, slamming through the oncoming waves with water rushing over its lee rail. Shock was being transmitted through its long hull and Marci felt it in the steering wheel and in her booted feet. The boat was thrumming with violence.

Swagwoman was doing everything she asked. The sea trials underway were a great success. She could hardly wait to report back to her grandfather and his boatyard. *A winner*.

* * *

Marci stiffened, hands white-knuckled on the wheel.

Something was wrong.

From her windward side came a low rumble, like that of a

freight train, a sound that grew louder and clearer, even above the fury of the storm.

She glanced about, trying to figure out the noise. And there it was. A monster wave, so big it was roaring over all the other waves.

"Mother of God!"

The rogue wave loomed high off her starboard beam. It was high—higher than her mast. And fast.

She spun the wheel furiously, rudders groaning and squealing, trying to turn her boat and head off.

The vessel accelerated furiously and teetered, balancing on the edge of survival. Then it canted dangerously as its deep fin keel bit into the roaring ocean, mast racing down toward the water.

Marci could feel the chill of the icy waters on her face.

The speeding hull reared up on one side and remained suspended for a moment or two, hesitating.

There was a dull cracking noise and the dark seas rushed up with terrible finality.

SECTION

ONE

THE

SEARCHERS

San Diego Harbor
Just Off Coronado Island

1

THE SCARRED WOODEN SAILBOAT surged gently in the harbor swells, halyards clanking gently in the freshening evening breeze. Kevlin Star was anchored in the sandy bottom off Hotel Coronado, the venerable San Diego Hotel, painted golden in the setting sun.

There was a low haze on the water and a warm layer of air that seemed to cling over the water—the sure start of a Pacific low. Something was stirring out in the vast reaches of the Pacific.

"*Perseverance...come in.*"

Big mistake, he realized. He had turned off his cell phone and pager to get some privacy. But he still had his ship's VHF radio monitoring marine calls —all good skippers do.

Obviously, he hadn't turned the damned thing off soon enough.

"Kev, go to channel 68."

What now? He adjusted the brim of his sun-bleached baseball cap, and keyed his mike.

"Bear? I just got my hook down."

"You finally got away for the weekend, right?" Kevlin could hear the low chuckle.

"Yeah, I'm gone." He had stopped at the old fishing pier and got two hot lobster sandwiches, extra mayo. A dill pickle.

Supper. Now growing cold.

Kevlin had been with the magazine almost six months, which is practically a lifetime in the hotly competitive boating magazine industry, and was used to getting calls at odd hours. Especially from Bear, the magazine's technical editor and ship communications officer, who delighted in hunting him down.

Usually with surprises.

"Listen up, Kev. Something bad is plowing through the Tasman Sea," Bear said. "The satellite stuff looks like a massive high pressure system is fighting with two low pressure systems and the low pressure system is winning."

"Are you on the net right now? Live?"

"True that. Looks nasty."

"Wait a minute. Two low-pressure systems? A couple of storms combining?"

"Remind you of something?"

The perfect storm, Tasman Sea style. Hurricane-force winds howling up from Antarctica, clawing the Tasman current the wrong way, filling the seas with steep black monsters.

Woe betide any poor sailor caught in their clutches.

Kevlin started getting that aw-shit feeling. "Did they get out a warning to mariners?"

"From the squawking I hear on the ham bands, nobody knew what was coming. The high hid the barometric warning until the storm actually hit. Then, boom."

The short answer was a quick no. A weather bomb that caught everyone by surprise. Sailors were out there right now, fighting for their lives in what might be the storm of the century.

Including one lone sailor he knew in a new, untested boat. On its first sea trials.

A big boat. In his opinion, too big for a little blonde to handle alone. And a damned racing machine at that.

Kevlin's stomach did a flip. He shoved his lobster sandwiches to one side, almost afraid to ask:

"Any report on Marci?"

Bear hesitated. "Thing is, Kev. She's gone missing."

2

8:36 P.M. Kevlin grunted apologetically as his old sailboat bumped noisily alongside the main gangway of the huge motor yacht.

He stole a glance at his Timex diving watch. He had made good time sailing across San Diego harbor to *Corinthian II*, moored in Santa Del Rio marina of Harbor Island, not far from the old America's Cup racer compounds. The 260-foot, tri-deck motor yacht, aka the "wedding cake," was the floating office of *Megasail* magazine.

He bounded up the boarding ladder two steps at a time, dashing into the big ship's communication's center on the top level, whose cabin top sprouted a small forest of antennas, revolving disks and satellite dishes. Inside the center, computer displays glowed warmly and three radios squawked long-distance reception.

"Yo, Bear," Kevlin hollered.

He waited a moment, glancing about the room: near one desk were a partially opened pizza, and, a half-drunk cup of latte in a glass container.

Bear was in his den all right. But where?

Bear's scraggly reddish beard, and thatch-like hair lent credence to his nickname, as did his bear-like lurch. Amiable in all other matters, he permitted no levity in his chosen love, electronics, or in his "toys." These were strictly off limits.

Kevlin put his index finger on the nearest sideband radio and deliberately turned the digital tuning frequency. The dialogue began to blur then squeal.

From a corner of the room, up popped a massive head, one hand pulling off ancient radio headset. His hobby radio. Wordlessly, Bear padded over to the errant radio and delicately adjusted the dial.

Only after the transmission resumed did his small, gray eyes flick to the intruder.

"Kev, I told you never to do that," he said patiently.

"Good to see you too, old buddy," Kevlin said. "I figured you'd like to know I'm here."

"No worries there. *Everybody* knows you're here." Bear shook his head. "I can practically sell tickets to people who want to see you crash land *Leaky Teaky*." He chuckled.

"One and done." Kevlin shrugged. "Anything new?

"Take a gander at the satellite pictures. I just downloaded them." Bear spread out a series of fax copies of ultra-high level photographs with a weather chart showing concentric circles getting closer together. "Hurricane winds. High seas."

A momentary vision came to Kevlin of Marci out there alone, gamely fighting the wheel of her huge racer. "Can we pick up her radio transmissions?"

Bear spread his hands, apologetically. "Nada."

"Team Australia?" Kevlin hoped her home base would have something.

"Their web site's slow to update —as usual, they got the least the last."

That figured. Team Australia would be frantically trying to get in touch with *Swagwoman* and probably fending off unwelcome queries. Updating their web site and answering looky-loos would not be their top priority.

"Anything from the Sydney Coast Guard?"

"Some transmissions from boats caught in the storm. A couple calling Mayday."

"But not Marci?"

"Have some coffee," Bear said, pointing to his ever-present espresso maker. "We can try some more frequencies and connections."

Bear was putting him off, so he had to inquire: "Officially or unofficially?"

"Whatever." Bear said, with an air of impatience to get going. "Before I forget. Sam wants you." Sam was the magazine publisher and the owner of the boat.

"She's on board? A little more good news to brighten my day?"

"No doubt she may have heard you come in." Bear sat down in

his no-arms secretarial chair before his main computer, staring at the monitor. He began typing on the buff-colored keyboard, at first a few keys at a time, then with increasing fury.

"Whatcha going after?"

Bear glanced up with a look that was reserved for lesser mortals. He was attempting a low-level hack, trying to get into a secure site by bypassing the identification code. Bear was a part of the hacker cult of southern California, amateurs who secretly passed around codes and passwords to enter forbidden computer sites — mostly for the gleeful joy of it and to prove they were smarter than the "suits." Some, like Bear, had advanced code-breaking software and access to the computers that could use them. Also slightly illegally.

"The news behind the news?"

"Somebody's got to hear something, know something at this point, Kev."

"I figure the Internet's buzzing."

"Always is." He stopped typing, raising one hand in warning. "Wait a sec, Kev. I'm getting something."

"Oh, Christ..." Kevlin leaned closer to the screen, catching the scrolling message.

"..new racer *Jolly Swagwoman*."

"That's her. Marci. What've you got into?

"Sydney Coast Guard, " Bear hushed him, his fingers scrolling down the screen, "Their private message board. Shut up a second!"

"...in its first sea trails appeared to be experiencing radio transmission difficulties, then logged no further contact with shore.

"Shit."

"Her approximate location was near the epicenter of the developing storm system at 1630 hours. Her team has had no further communications from the vessel and they are formally requesting search and rescue operations begin immediately."

"That's it?" Kevlin could hardly believe the brevity of the report.

Bear twirled the dials. "That's the latest. Maybe there'll be more on the Internet."

Kevlin swallowed hard. A boat like Marci's would have all

sorts of sensors over its hull and mast, automatically broadcasting data back to Team Australia. That would include information
on the boat's speed, its sailing conditions, and, especially its
exact GPS location. Something should have been coming through.

But all communications, including voice radio calls from
Marci as well as the automatic streaming sensor data, had ceased.

He glanced at Bear's computer display of world time zones.
1630 hours was....six hours ago.

Kevlin winced. No wonder they called in the Coast Guard.
They must be getting worried.

An invisible fist slammed into his gut.

Now, so was he.

*   *   *

There was a gust of air-conditioned air. Sam glared unblinking
from the open doorway. In the confined space of the cabin she
towered — all five feet of her.

Samantha "Sam" Traveler, the magazine's publisher and the
boat owner, had obviously been in the ship's exercise room.
Sweat streamed down her high cheekbones, but her dark eyes
were cold and flat. She was not happy.

He harbored a healthy respect for her, composed of equal
amounts of instinctive wariness and the fact that she was his
boss.

He had the feeling that not only was he new and expendable
but that he had an expiration date stamped on his forehead. Sam
had hired him from an Eastern boating magazine after she had
seen his prestigious Boating Writers International writing awards.
The Dragon Lady made it clear she wanted him to get awards for
her magazine. She was still waiting.

"Just coming to see you," Kevlin tensed.

"R-i-g-h-t." The DL's eyes said no.

In another time, another place, she could have been called
beautiful. "Kill the cover."

She tossed a copy of the magazine's front cover at the radio
stack. It landed with a whump. Bear jumped.

"Why the hell for?"

Her dark eyes glittered, but her mouth twisted up in a small sardonic grin. Obviously, she was hardly challenged. "How about, 'cause I said so.'"

Yeah, the DL's command voice. Kevlin's eyes cut over to Bear, who glanced away. It was obvious that Bear had been in touch with the boss, but had not told him.

Marci was on the magazine cover—featuring his article on the comely Marci and her lone-girl ocean racer. It was a sure-fire BWI award winner, he figured. One of his best stories. .

"All we know is that Marci hasn't reported in, Kevlin said, "I'm concerned, but my best guess is she's probably still out there."

"Our magazine just went to the printers—and our cover story's already out of date."

"Hey, there are a hundred things that could have gone wrong out there. Her batteries went out, or, the antennas got blown off. Somebody'll find her."

"Wrong cover, wrong time."

"We don't know that yet."

Sam moved forward, pointing her finger at him "Well, we can't just sit here with our fingers up our tushes—doing nothing. Am I not making myself clear?"

Kevlin paced the floor, his stomach doing flip flops. Something was very near and he felt it. His neck was on the line. He needed to come up with something.

He said, "We can change some stuff on the cover type or the inside story. A box. A sidebar story. A quick update. We still got a little time, either way things play out, and we'd still be covered. Good to go."

"We're monitoring all transmissions…" Bear began.

Sam pinned Kevlin with a glare and leaned in. Her lips barely moved. "DSDQ." That meant, do something, damned quick.

*   *   *

He slammed the cabin door behind him and stepped out onto the deck, looking westward.

He shivered involuntarily. The breeze off the sea had an odd feel to it.

He didn't like it at all. And that was not all he didn't like.

3

OUTSIDE THE CABIN WINDOW, night had turned to day. Below him stretched the vast panorama of the Tasman Sea. From this height, between breaks in the cloud cover, it looked blue and inviting.

But Kevlin knew better. The flecks of white on the tiny waves were whitecaps—huge, storm-tossed seas.

Marci could be anywhere down there.

He shifted uncomfortably in his seat. He had caught the next flight to Australia and only had time to grab his sea bag. He opted for a first class ticket. The Dragon Lady wanted action, and now she was getting it on her dime. She'd find out about the extra cost early next week.

He'd have to come up with something. That was the scary part.

His weary mind began to sort through the problems of a lone racer at sea in a brand new sailboat, on its first sea trials.

Anything could have gone wrong, literally.

New boats are prone to have problems and usually follow Murphy's law of the sea: things go wrong when you least expect them and at the worst possible times.

And in the most unexpected places.

Electrical problems would head the list and posed the simplest explanation. A single splash of seawater could have cut out her boat's complex combination of 12 and 24-volt electrical systems.

Ah, yes, he mused unhappily. Racers were notorious for being part submarine—some water always got below and shorted something out. With no electricity, Marci couldn't use her radio. That would account for why Team Australia hadn't heard from her.

Too easy. Kevlin adjusted himself in his seat as another thought came to him. She'd still have her EPIRB—the emergency position finder. It was waterproof, hand-held, and had its own batteries; you used it if you were in deep trouble. A high-powered satellite signal would broadcast your position, who you were, and, hopefully, a rescuer would be on the way.

But there had been only silence. There was no signal.

He glanced down once more at the Tasman Sea. In the big waves down there, it would not be too difficult for a hot-handed racer like Marci to stuff a boat into one of those monsters, get swallowed up and not come back. Her boat could have twisted out of control and capsized.

Or pitch poled—the nightmare of being tossed end over end.

Kevlin was sweating. Marci was a real fire-in-the belly winner on the brutal ocean-racing circuit—a rising heroine in a country that idolized sailors. The Aussie Press had dubbed her their "Golden Girl"— *Gee Gee* for short. A real pop star.

Storm or no storm, Marci would carry as much sail as long as she could to test the boat and probe its weaknesses. He hoped she hadn't found the latter.

But this was the golden age of racing. Now in the start of the 1990s, people not only sailed around the world, but a dauntless few actually raced their boats. They carried sail long after they should have taken down canvas. Or even heaved to.

Boats overturned, boats broke, people got dumped in the water, but—incredibly— no one got hurt. Or killed.

So far.

Marci's face on *Megasail's* cover haunted him, with her wide blue eyes, slightly cocked eyebrows and warm, intelligent look, sometimes a little on the bold side, when she looked at him. A generous mouth, blonde hair done up smartly in a pony tail, with strands of bangs forever wisping out from beneath her baseball cap.

God, but he missed her.

A shudder shook the plane and Kevlin had to grip the sides of his seat. Warning chimes sounded; a red light flashed on. In front of him, a man spilled his cup of coffee. A woman yelped.

Back to reality. "Fasten your seat belts," the steward's voice was apathetic. "We're experience some in-air turbulence."

The 747 began its long descent into the maelstrom.

Sydney, and maybe some answers, lay below.

4

K EVLIN ANXIOUSLY made his way through the deplaning line, glad to be off the airplane and on solid ground. There was a milling, noisy crowd at the gate.

But where was his man?

He glanced about. From about the third row of people, someone was waving a camera in the air. All he could see was a hand and a black Nikon.

Yes. Kevlin strode forward.

Waiting for him, but looking as if he'd swallowed something bad, was Bruce Laughlin-Taylor.

The photographer was short, but wiry looking, dressed in his usual khaki cottons, bush jacket and hat, a flash of colored silk at the neck, despite the heat. The shorts only emphasized Kevlin's impression that the man had the spindliest legs he'd ever seen. The magazine stringer's left eye had a startling intensity, but his right was lazy, sometimes cocking toward a broken aquiline nose. Neither eye looked very happy.

"G'day," Kevlin said.

Bruce rolled his good eye in exasperation.

For many years, Bruce had been the Sydney stringer for *Megasail.* He probably started steaming the moment Sam sent him an e-mail or faxed him.

Or, knowing the DL and Bear, and considering Brucey, probably both.

"I'll give it to you short and straight," Bruce said. "Nada. Search and bloody Rescue didn't have a fix on *Swagwoman's* last heading and speed—she was going like a bat out of hell, by the way—before Marci's electronics conked out."

" That leaves a lot of sea room to get lost in."

"They started at scratch by running the last known coordinates—relayed hours earlier—of *Swagwoman* through their computers."

"Figuring in the storm winds, and direction, that'd give them some idea of where the boat went."

Bruce cut him short. "They don't know whether she is under storm sail or not—whether she finally decided to heave to—or was at some point overwhelmed in the storm and is just drifting. Or in a life raft."

"Hundreds of miles off her last known position."

Bruce snorted. "Considering the variables, actually, *thousands* of square miles."

Kevlin frowned. Marci had blasted out of the Sydney heads into the Tasman Sea and then changed to a southerly heading, wringing out her new racer. On a fast boat, how far had she gotten? She was headed toward the desolate southern Indian Ocean, one of the most inaccessible spots imaginable on the face of the earth. Even modern aircraft with black boxes and big ships have been lost there forever..

Bruce continued: "They have three P3 Orions out on a grid search with their radar."

"Only three planes?"

"Military. But civilian planes are also being brought in since other boats got caught and are in trouble: *Lady Mine* capsized. *Slim Jimmy* was taking on water. Search and Rescue went with their chopper to take off the captain and crews. They barely made it back."

"She could still be out there."

"We got a choice? Maybe something will turn up."

"Big help!" Kevlin began stalking out of the airport. "What's Tremain up to? Is he just *waiting,* too?"

Tremain Whitman was the Australian boat builder of *Jolly Swagwoman* and head of the Australian racing syndicate backing Marci.

"Ease up, mate. He was the one to call in Search and Rescue."

"Why'd he delay so long?"

"Sweet Jesus, he didn't *know,* either. It's a bloody riddle. But now he's getting anything that'll float or fly out for a look-see. Formed his own rescue net. Yachts, commercial freighters, fishing boats, private planes. Anything."

Kevlin had an image of a wet and chilled Marci, cursing the heavens as the hours wore on. He sensed something had happened out there: a failure of rigging, the mainsheet jammed, something went out.

Maybe she was not on her boat.

If Marci had to go to her inflatable, and was riding out the storm in that, the Tasman Sea could be an especially evil, wicked place.

He swallowed hard. "Did you get me in to see Tremain?"

Bruce hesitated. "Reporters have been circling him like vultures. He wasn't thrilled to learn that another one was arriving."

"Did he remember me?" Kevlin was suddenly wary.

"He didn't say. I didn't ask. But you're on with him. In his boat yard."

"When?"

"Soon as you get there." Bruce shrugged his shoulders apologetically.

Kevlin let it pass.

5

THE DAY WAS BLUSTERY, with high winds off the harbor. Sharp gusts shook Bruce's old Jaguar as it took a hard right turn to the waterfront. Far off, on a white-capped harbor, the ferry to Pinchgut chugged away toward Circular Quay.

The boat yard was located in the south of the harbor and was announced by a series of docks and a fenced-in security area. A powerful lift crane, with a cruising boat in its slings, reared over the sailboats moored along the sturdy wooden docks.

Bruce skidded to a halt. They strode quickly over the wind-swept planks to a fenced-in area, identified only by a hand-carved wooden sign, that announced, *Great Barrier Reef Boats, Tremain Whitman, Prop.* Beyond was a weed-choked tangle of rigging and masts surrounding the hulks of fiberglass molds.

Inside was a different story. The interior of the boat shop was meticulously organized and neat as a hospital's operating room. Fluorescent fixtures and overhead skylights bathed the shop in sparkling luminescence. Tools hung glistening in rows; workers moved among them like surgeons in white.

Overlooking all was a second-story office, small and wooden, furnished with well-worn, dented and scratched steel desks, probably military surplus, each bearing a high-powered computer. Along the walls were thumb tacked rows of boat blueprints, with the oddity of a rustic, hand-carved wooden cross.

The back of the room glowed and hummed with more computers, electronic displays, high-powered radios, printers and fax machines. Here and there were headsets with microphones. A speaker blurred and rasped. Obviously, a communications center.

A young blonde at the front desk glanced up momentarily. She started to smile a greeting at Bruce.

When she saw Kevlin, her face froze.

"G'day. We're here for the interview," Bruce announced cheerily.

Her eyes snapped disapproval.

He shot an inquiring glance at Bruce. No help there. When he turned back, she had disappeared into the back office.

She popped out. "You can go in now."

She was still staring at him. *What was it?*

He took a deep breath, brushed past her and walked into the paneled office. She watched him all the way through the doorway.

A big man with the short-cut white hair glanced up from his computer screen. A scowl grew on his craggy face.

"Yes, sir.." Kevlin walked forward, holding out his hand. "We have an appointment."

"You!" Tremain thundered, crossing his arms and ignoring Kevlin's outstretched hand. "I was supposed to meet a *Megasail* editor. Nobody told me *who*."

He glared at Bruce, who took two steps back. "No wonder I smelled a rat."

Kevlin stiffened, withdrawing his hand. He glanced toward Bruce. Again, no help.

"Sir, I flew a long way to meet you."

"You just have. G'bye."

"If I could have just a few minutes..."

"No time. I've got a search going on."

"I'm sorry, sir. Look, it's not just the magazine. I want to help Marci."

"Out!" Tremain thundered.

"But I need to..."

"Out! Get out!"

6

DARKNESS HAD FALLEN, but Bruce still was driving his old Jaguar like a madman down the twisting, ill-lighted waterfront. Wisps of fog blew in, obscuring the cobbled streets. Kevlin braced himself in the leather seat, trying to hold back his frustration.

"I thought that went well, considering," offered Bruce.

"Considering what?" Kevlin growled. "Marci's missing. Tremain's saying squat. The magazine's still hanging open on deadline. I'd say, considering, that the home team isn't having too good a day."

"Considering," Bruce drawled.

A burst of wind hit the Jag, sagging it to one side on its worn shocks. Bruce corrected by stamping on the accelerator. The car howled, speeded up, tires moaning in a turn.

"Deadline," Kevlin growled louder. "Coming up fast. Dammit, Bruce. You're our man down here!"

There was a laconic pause, as if some recognition had just been passed.

Bruce spun the wheel; the Jaguar took a hard left and clattered over the wooden planking of a pier. Bruce brightened. " Time we met someone at my office — right about now."

Fishing boats groaned at their fenders in the high winds on the darkened wharf; mist swirled in billows around the harbor lights. In front of them, a red neon light with broken letters blinked out *The Old Sailor's Home*.

"We're here!" Bruce said delightedly. The Jag skidded to a halt.

*   *   *

The stench of the bar engulfed Kevlin: old beer, cheap whisky and bad cigars. It was difficult to see in the dim atmosphere. A scarred mahogany bar ran down one side, opposite a row of high-backed wooden booths.

The Old Sailor's Home was clearly a hard-drinking boiler-maker joint for sailors, fishermen and waterfront workers. Kevlin's eyes began to water.

Bruce moved briskly to the end booth. A sign thumb tacked to the wall above it announced, "Reserved."

He spread his arms expansively. "My office, mate!"

"You've outdone yourself, mate." Sydneysiders were not the only ones who could be laid back when they wanted to be.

A lamp stuck out of the woodwork and shone feebly on the table. Under a telephone were torn pieces of paper, with writing in pencil addressed to Bruce.

"The usual, Brucey?"

"Yeah," Bruce said to the spike-haired waitress. "Any messages for me?"

"You got a bloke at the bar." She tossed her head in his direction. "He's been there a while." She turned to Kevlin: "And you?"

Bruce held up his hand. "He'll have one, too."

"Right. Two green beers."

"Hold on," Kevlin protested, but she trotted off and minutes later, arrived holding up two foaming glasses of greenish liquid.

Bruce raised his glass in a toast: "Through the lips and over the gums, oh fuck — here it comes."

"What's this stuff?"

"It's a shot of Rose's Lime Juice in a Foster's Beer. Smile. Drink up," he warned quietly, "Don't attract attention. It's either beer, boilermakers, or whiskey down here. "

"Who's your contact?" Kevlin took a sip. Green beer wasn't bad.

"Andy McGlaughlin." Bruce signaled the beefy bartender, who, in turn, nodded to a man at the end of the bar.

A man in sun bleached jeans with holes in the knees, sweat-stained work shirt and lace-up boots picked up his boilermaker— a beer in one hand, a tumbler of whisky in the other—and shuffled toward them. He bore himself stiffly upright, deliberately, as if his body were used to carrying a lot of weight.

He squinted his eyes warningly at Kevlin. "Who's he?"

"This here's Kevlin. A mate of mine," Bruce answered quickly.

"All we want is a little of your time."

"Yeah. Sure. Money?"

Bruce pulled out some bills. "We know you did an underwater deal."

"That's my business. I'm a diver." The man counted slowly.

Bruce continued: "We need a little information, like, who hired you?"

"Couldn't say. They didn't tell me, you know."

"One of the racing syndicates?"

"They wanted some snaps done on *Jolly Swagwoman*."

"In dry dock?"

"They guard that too close. In the water."

Underwater pictures. Kevlin leaned forward. If the diver had actual underwater photographs, that could be a real breakthrough. No one in the press had seen the secret keel or underbody.

The diver's face darkened with anger. "I didn't get that far."

"That compound was fenced all the way to the bottom of the water." Bruce said suspiciously. "How'd you get in?"

"I used a circulating rebreather, so no bubbles showed. Came in late one afternoon, when the sun was at my back and the blokes on guard would get their eyes blinded by the glare.

"And the steel fence?"

"Cut my way inside. I was OK till I heard alarm bells going off—you'd be surprised at how loud those bloody sheilas came through the water.

"They had the compound wired..."

"Tight security. Sensors all over the place. I was made, so I took off."

"No pictures."

The diver permitted himself a mean smile. "But I saw it. A good look, up close. Not long, mind you." He paused for a sip of his boilermaker. "The underbody starts with a v shape, a soft chine up front, then gets long and flat, like a big dinghy. Wide, too. Especially at the stern."

"...everybody's figured that."

"But the keel... *that's* different." The diver grew respectful. He rocked back and forth as he thought about it. "Real different."

"How so?"

"Hard to explain..."

"I have an idea." Kevlin said. "Can you draw?"

"This is for money, right? "

Kevlin nodded and the diver muttered, "then I damned well can draw something." He took the money.

From a nearby container, the diver grabbed a white napkin, and spread it apart. Slowly and intently, his head cocked slightly to one side, the diver began to draw. Kevlin leaned forward. The diver sketched first a side view and then a front view. It was a surprisingly draftsman like rendering.

"Dimensions?" Kevlin asked.

He shrugged his shoulders, thought a moment. "I can esti-mate," he said, adding some figures and pushed the napkin toward Bruce.

"So that's it!" Kevlin inhaled sharply. "The keel! Anybody else know?"

The diver shook his head. "The bloke who hired me got pissed when I didn't get the photos."

" No pix, no money?"

"The bastard started to chew me down. I told him to fuck off."

"So they don't know?" Kevlin's eyes glittered.

"I walked. But then I put two and two together and that's when I started looking for you, Brucey. I figured you'd find a way to fence the info for me."

"Hey, wait a minute. We need more than this..."

"It's a done deal." The diver took a last gulp of his boiler-maker and slammed down his whiskey glass upside down. He lumbered off.

*   *   *

"Conniving bastard!" Bruce's good eye blinked.

"Look at this!" Kevlin's finger traced the outline of the diver's drawing.

"So *that's* the secret keel." Bruce hunched forward. "A deep fin with a flattened torpedo bulb shape to keep the ballast weight low."

"And the trailing edge looks like it has a vortex tip to reduce turbulence, so she'll slip along."

"The fin is...knife-like. Really deep, too."

"Damned thin — almost fragile looking —for a racer."

"Something up top, too. A slot.

"For some kind of mechanism?"

"Not like any I've seen."

"Why the long groove? What's it attached to?"

Bruce slowly shook his head. "I tell you this, mate. I wouldn't want to meet up with a Tasman Sea buster with *that* thing under me."

7

IT WAS MORNING in Sydney harbor. As light streamed in from the hatch above his bunk, the hull rolled back and forth in the high wind.

Kevlin lifted an eyelid and groaned.

A glance at his watch told him it was late morning and he remembered he had been invited aboard Bruce's rusty old steel schooner to bunk overnight in the crew's quarters.

Where to begin? He had struck out with Tremain Whitman —-his main hope. The diver's story was interesting, but proved nothing. Marci was still missing.

Back to square one. No story. And with a beaut of a hangover.

"*Kevlin.*" The voice boomed out from somewhere on deck.

He grabbed his jeans, slipped his feet, sockless, into a pair of old deck shoes and clambered up the hatchway. His head hurt; his stomach was queasy.

The gusts from the harbor greeted him. It was a raw day, he realized, as he tried to steady himself.

"Over here!" Bruce was beside the main mast, re tying a loose mainsail halyard. "I've been up for hours," he said, grinning. "If you can skip your morning tea and crumpets, I've something for you."

Kevlin winced at the thought of food.

Bruce dropped easily to the deck and peered at him. "Feeling a little bit under, mate?"

"Jet lag. That's all."

In truth, Kevlin had not matched Bruce drink for drink last night, carefully holding back—he thought. But this morning, Kevlin felt horribly hung over. Probably a combination of green beers and that monumental twenty-some hour flight.

"Some news," Bruce cheerfully announced. "Tremain's boat-yard has the New Zealand boat, *Kiwi Kubed.*"

Kevlin tried to appear interested.

"She's just finished her qualifying run for the big race and she's getting last-minute refitting, including new carbon fiber rudders. Now they want to do a quick sea trial. Wring her out a bit."

"Standard stuff." Kevlin's head hurt. He was feeling green.

"So, fancy this: one of the yard workers got sick last night at the tavern. Spent the night on the dunny. You know, the throne."

Kevlin managed a lop-sided grin: "The same guy you were buying boilermakers for? With the green beers?"

Bruce ignored the question: "He was supposed to be the crew for Morrison today on the test sail."

"Ain't gonna make it?"

Bruce smiled triumphantly: "So I arranged with ... a friend ... in Tremain's office to have a replacement go along."

"Uh, yeah. So...?" Kevlin stared unblinkingly. Reality was dawning.

"Sweet Jesus." Bruce rolled his eyes skyward. "*You'll* be going out for sea trials. You know, she's a sister ship to *Jolly Swagwoman*."

"The same?"

"I hear the keel's different. But same hull, same rig, with twin rudders."

Kevlin steadied himself. It was a superb opportunity.

He smiled but his stomach kept doing a lurching dance. It'd be great if he could keep from spending his time hanging over the lee rail.

*   *   *

Bruce handled the dinghy's oars expertly in the crosswinds. Off in the distance, on the harbor's north shore, was the Sydney Harbor Bridge, and further, the famous Opera House.

As they neared the New Zealand sailboat, Kevlin's first impression was that the racer was simply too large for any one sailor to handle, with her enormous sail plan and complex gear. Her mast seemed to spear into the sky.

A gust of wind caught her tall, black mast. She seemed to shiver in the water.

"Big, isn't she?" Bruce was pleased with himself.

When Kevlin did not respond, he continued: "*Kiwi Kubed* is a lot like *Jolly Swagwoman*. She should give you a good feel for what Marci's racer handled like."

"Might be something," Kevlin agreed, looking the huge racer over.

She lay close to the water, with low freeboard. She'd be a wet brute in rough seas — every wave she couldn't go over she'd plow through. Water would roar down the low decks. Right back at him and his tender tummy.

She was the vaunted ocean-going Racing 60 with the Century-class mast.

What Marci drove.

*   *   *

"Ahoy, the *Kubed*," Bruce shouted loud enough to make Kevlin's head hurt. "Prepare to accept boarders."

"Ahoy yourself," came a good-natured drawl with a New Zealand accent. "Here to see what a real boat looks like?"

As they climbed on board, Bruce whispered to Kevlin, "Morrison is a good shipwright and yard man. But I have to warn you: there are two opinions on his sailing abilities. His — and the rest of the world's." He smiled a conspiratorial smile.

Morrison appeared to be in his late 40's, a wiry, short sun-baked man wearing a striped tee shirt and oversized knee-length shorts. On his head was a wide-brimmed bush hat.

"Going out for sea trials?" Bruce gently inquired.

Morrison brushed his face. "Buggered if I know. I'm still waiting for my crew."

"D'you know I've been chatting with the boatyard. Your crew didn't show up there, either."

"Sick or something?"

"But you're all set now." Bruce winked in Kevlin's direction. "This here's your replacement. Name's Kevlin."

"Lord preserve us," Morrison said, squinting at Kevlin. "You look like hell, son."

"I ran into a bad batch of beer last night. But I've sailed before," Kevlin said. "Mostly I'm a small boat sailor."

Morrison considered his options. They appeared to be limited: zero or none. He made his choice.

"Well, we might as well have a go at it. Prepare to get this beast underway."

He peered down at Bruce. "You coming?"

Bruce's one good eye opened wide, the other started wandering. "Got things to do." He scuttled crab-like to his dinghy.

"Catch you later!" Bruce called out as he hastily rowed away. "By the by, I'm going to look into that matter we talked about last night. Ta."

What? Kevlin waved foggily from the cockpit.

Pleased with himself, Morrison slid behind the wheel. "Cast off," he commanded.

"Aye, skipper." That much he could do.

Kevlin felt the wind grab at the tall mast, heeling the vessel and sending vibrations to the rigging.

He inhaled deeply. His stomach lurched a little. The fresh sea air and the excitement were helping him recover.

"Sorry our little friend isn't coming along," Morrison said. "He'd have the ride of his miserable life to remember."

Then he laughed.

8

THE HUGE BOOM slammed back and forth in the harbor gusts, as if in anticipation of the blue-water ride that was to come.

Perspiring greatly, Kevlin cranked on the hand-powered winch. He did not count the time it took to get the mainsail up, but he guessed that it must be about 25 minutes.

Ow! He was hurting already.

The boat trembled as the mainsail began to shape itself up the mast. The wind machine was in its element, coming alive.

"Big, ain't she?" Morrison was enjoying himself hugely. Morrison was at the wheel; Kevlin was crewing. That meant he was doing most of the work.

Kevlin wrestled the oversized mainsheet and adjusted the traveler. The sail grew bar taut and the boat dove its lee rail into the white foam, accelerating.

Kevlin's knees nearly buckled; his stomach lurched. The sea was up; it was going to be a brutal ride.

God, he hated racing sailboats. Damned overpowered monsters. Beasts. How did Marci ever get hooked on them?

"Now the jib!" Morrison commanded.

Kevlin began pulling the jib halyard and suddenly, the wind had the headsail, tossing it about. It went up quickly. It was a shimmering gossamer of high-tech fabric, unfolding like an angel's wing.

Bam. Kevlin felt as if the huge racer was about to lift off the water.

"Take the wheel," Morrison said. "Steady as she goes." He stepped to one side to get a better view of the instrumentation.

A lob of green water roared back along the deck. Kevlin clutched the helm with both hands and braced himself. The roller slugged him, soaking his clothing. Salt water stung his eyes; he forgot about his stomach. He shook his head, clearing his vision.

"You've been properly baptized," Morrison yelled, laughing.

*   *   *

Soon they were out past the protective Sydney Heads, a tight entrance to the huge harbor, and were heading to the Tasman Sea.

The bow was dancing up, over, and into the white-capped ocean waves, sending back columns of water and tons of spray. It was wet work, pushing the boat to windward.

The sails grew taut as steel in the heavy wind; the sailboat dug her shoulder further into the sea. In the stern, the long, thin carbon rudders bit deep; below, the deep keel strained to keep the racer upright. Starboard side stanchions and lifelines disappeared under white water.

"Ready?" Morrison yelled above the whine in the rigging and the crashing of the waves. He was enjoying himself. "Time to find out what she'll do!"

"We're hitting 19...now 20 knots," Kevlin shouted.

The boat's bounding motion changed into jarring menace. The racer was flexing its muscles.

"Twenty two now! And *gaining*."

The boat shook with power, the mast flexing every time the bow caught a wave. The world was blurring motion, vibration, water and sunlight. It was like being in a washing machine.

Kevlin gritted his teeth, his feet wide apart in the cockpit, bracing himself. In his hands the wheel vibrated with pressure as the rudders sliced deep.

This was the wettest, meanest boat he'd ever been on. *Poor Marci!*

A wave reared up and smashed into the hull. The boat staggered, then heeled. White water poured into the cockpit and from somewhere came a noise like a cracking board. Then another.

The boat spun around, dangerously fast.

"What was that?" Kevlin shouted. "Did we hit something?"

"Get her back on course!" Morrison shouted, hanging onto a stanchion. There was fear in his voice.

Waves slammed broadside; solid water climbed the deck as Kevlin wrestled with the wheel. "Nothing's happening!"

"She'll *capsize*. Get the pressure off!"

But Morrison was already at the mainsail, his hand fluttering at the winch. He cranked. Again. Once more.

But the sail would not come down. "Stuck!"

"Try to hand reef," Kevlin yelled. The boat shook, beginning to capsize. Morrison grabbed the mast and hung there.

Freight trains of water slammed into the hull, covering the deck. The bow was rearing wildly. The spray felt like buckshot.

"Morrison!" But the foreman was frozen, his mouth wide. He would be no use at the mast.

"Get back and take over the wheel," Kevlin shouted.

Bruce had been right: Morrison was more of a yard bird than a blue-water sailor. Kevlin also noted Morrison was no longer so smug.

"I'll try the jib." Kevlin snapped his safety harness into a jack-stay, dropped to his hands and knees, and crawled along the thin stainless steel safety line. Above him, the huge jib flogged madly in the wind above him, threatening to tear itself apart, and maybe him, if he'd let it.

The boat tore into a wave, and plunged underwater.

He lunged for the rail, missed it, and felt himself carried over the side in the mass of green water. The huge hull knifed past him like a giant scimitar.

He went under again. A sharp pain stabbed around his safety harness, yanking him along the wave under the flashing green.

He tried to pull himself up, but the wave pressure was too great. He was powerless. The bow went down and he went flying, still tethered to the boat.

Then he was on deck again, sputtering. Squinting, he could only see white foam everywhere, but no boat. The mast broke free, then part of the deck burst into view.

Scrabbling frantically between waves, he wedged himself into the pulpit and held his breath. The bow dove again, and he was plastered down by the weight of the water. It seemed to be forever, but as he rose to the surface, he frantically began pulling down the jib by hand. It was slow, hard work, but gradually he felt the press of canvas reduced.

The big vessel's heel lessened and slowly the boat began to right itself. He left a patch of jib up. It would have to do.

But in these waves, the boat was slewing about, dangerously out of control. If one of the monsters should catch her broadside, she'd roll over 180 degrees. A full capsize.

Shaky and shivering, Kevlin worked his way back to the cockpit as quickly as he could. Morrison still clung to the helm.

"What the hell happened?" Kevlin yelled.

Morrison's face twitched nervously as he gave the wheel a spin. It revolved effortlessly in his hand. "Damn me," he said, pathetically, "if we haven't lost our rudders." The foreman shook his head in incredulous disbelief.

Kevlin stepped forward to flip switches. No radio—no power.

"Bloody bitch!" Morrison suddenly screamed, kicking the useless steering wheel. "Damn, damn, damn."

Kevlin looked up at the mast, bending in the gusts. The mainsail was slatting, booming like a cannon; the boat was doing a slam dance in the waves.

"We got a hull and we got wind, so we're basically OK," he announced to Morrison, "We'll use sails. And sail pressure. And something else."

"What for?"

"To steer us."

Morrison's face twitched and his eyes grew large.

"No worries," Kevlin said, adjusting the traveler and easing out some of the mainsheet. The boat heeled in a burst of wind, and straightened up. Kevlin wrapped the jib sheet around one of the massive winches, tightening the hank of jib he had left up. He cleated off the sheets. He'd have to use the grinders again.

The bow hesitated, then began to swing about. The mainsail banged noisily over. They were turned around and running downwind. But without control.

Kevlin jumped below looked about the cabin. There, under a partition, was his prize. Gingerly, he loosened it from its resting place, then tied on two stout nylon lines to the handle.

Morrison's eyes popped: "The dunny bucket? The poop pail?

Yes. Kevlin wrapped each line around the boat's side winches. Then he threw the heavy metal bucket overboard.

"It's a drogue," yelled Kevlin. "Poop bucket steering."

As it submerged, the heavy galvanized steel bucket slowed the boat slightly, maybe half a knot. But now it was time for the test

as he winched on one line. The drogue obediently slid in the wake
to one side. The boat changed course. Tension on the other line,
the boat changed again.

"I don't bloody well believe it!" Morrison twitched, his eyes
wide.

*   *   *

Even under reduced sail, the racer plowed massively through
the waves, steered by the pressure on her sails and her improvised
drogue. She was a wild and slewing steed, barely under control.

"Harbor entryway dead ahead!" Morrison's face twitched.

Kevlin was perspiring heavily, concentrating on the big winches. This was the dangerous part. Without a rudder, total control
was impossible, an almost elusive goal. But he'd make it work.

They shot through the narrow Sydney Heads, racing in the
harbor, flying back like a homesick angel.

"We're coming in too hot," Morrison yelled, as the docks
neared. "She'll hole herself on a pier."

The sailboat flew into the final thousand yards. The boatyard
crew, alerted to the danger, was running down the dock. Tremain
lumbered angrily, waving his arms.

Kevlin dashed below, emerging a moment later, crouched over
a heavy burden. With a splash, Kevlin hurled his package overboard. Behind him a nylon line slid quickly into the water. He
cleated off one end.

"Let go the sheets!" Kevlin yelled. The big mainsail flapped
harmlessly in the wind, the huge jib was set free.

He glanced aft—the line was coming taut. As if caught in a
giant hand, the ship began to drag to a halt. By the time the boat
bumped against the docks, it was barely moving.

"One and done," Kevlin said as the dock crew grabbed the
bobbing hull.

"Where'd you learn that, mate?" someone shouted admiringly.

"Old California docking trick," Kevlin answered. "I tossed out
the ship's Danforth. The anchor held us like a brake."

Morrison slumped beside the wheel. "Let's do that again not
anytime soon."

Kevlin remembered the razzing he used to get back in San
Diego. Bear joked that he could practically sell tickets to see

Kevlin's docking of the *Leaky Teaky*.

Not today. Now when he needed to, he had precisely docked the giant racer. It was hard to believe that it was something he did with his own hands, so easily, when he needed to. He just reached inside himself and what he needed was already there.

It was so simple, so amazing a realization, it marked a turning point in his life. *To win, you first gotta try. He who tries, wins.*

From now on, he'd be trying, big time.

A wave of satisfaction rolled over his tired frame.

"By the way," he said to a puzzled Tremain, "You need a new poop bucket."

*   *   *

As he walked down the wooden pier, Kevlin was caught up in his new-found insights. He could empathize for diminutive Marci raising that huge mainsail in about 25 minutes of hard cranking. He certainly felt the strain, crank after crank of the halyard winch, and it was downright painful after the first 10 minutes.

Then she'd have to go forward to hoist the huge jib by hand. He was practically exhausted before he took the wheel.

And she'd have to take that beast out for a sail, not just for a few hours, as he had done in the sea trials, but for days on end. And in the big race, for months— nonstop from port to port. Alone.

If the headsails needed changing in a storm, she'd have to go forward to fight the wind-mad sails. If the main needed reefing, she'd have to cling to the mast in a pitching, reeling boat.

The sheer physical energy she needed was phenomenal.

No wonder she was such a fitness buff. He remembered how he had met her at a Sydney gym, where she was also having a photo shoot — not his, which would be entirely onboard her boat. Here she was doing a local magazine shoot and getting paid a lot of money for it.

Gee Gee. The Golden Girl. The only girl racer.

He watched her as she worked out, arm curl after arm curl, then the squats, then squat jumps, then the abs.

"Let's see some abs, Marci," one of the cameramen called out, a little too merrily, Kevlin thought. "You got 'em. Show 'em."

Marci laughed, and then pulled up her T-top, curling it just

under her sports bra. Then she carefully lowered the top of her
workout pants, slowly, down the hips until they were nearly hori-
zontal across her body.

"You're still legal,"the photographer joked.

Marci grinned. She was a professional athlete, proud of her
well toned body. But then Kevlin noticed she looked down to
double check. The lowered pants didn't show anything.

That was OK. She lit up her model's smile and then clenched
her abs. They were spectacular.

"It's the isometrics," she said."When you're on a sailboat, you
constantly move back and forth. Gives your abs a real workout."

Kevlin agreed. Nice abs.

"Getting an eyeful?" she playfully tossed her blonde ponytail
about, like a cat switching its beautiful tail, moving from pose to
pose. First one hip was out; then the other. Flick. Flick.

Buns of steel. Isometrics helped there, too.

Kevlin didn't answer, but averted his eyes. He thought he saw
her smile at him.

"That's enough," she said to the photographer.

"Never enough, Marci."

"It'll have to do, mate." Marci waved them off and then adjusting her clothing. The end of the photo shoot meant she could get
back to her work as an athlete in a very athletic endeavor. The
photo shoots and the photo spreads paid the bills for fitting out
her racing boat. Everything went into that boat. It was a hole in
the water into which she threw money.

For *Megasail,* and the cover story Kevlin was here to do, she
was all properly decked out as a yachtswoman, in her foulies,
with her baseball cap on below her hood. She had her racing
goggles atop her head, perched there like sunglasses. She smiled
beguilingly. At him.

Kevlin took a deep breath, and then let it out slowly.

Her face on the *Megasail* cover haunted him, with her wide
blue eyes, slightly cocked eyebrows and warm, intelligent look,
sometimes a little on the bold side when she looked at him.
Awesome.

God but he missed her, terribly. *Where the hell was she?*

9

A BOUT AN HOUR LATER, a boat thumped lightly alongside Bruce's old schooner. Kevlin was slumped in the navigation room with the single sideband radio tuned in to the search
going on for *Jolly Swagwoman*. There were light footsteps on the
deck. Someone peered carefully down into the darkened cabin.
Framed in the sunlight, her golden hair cascaded lightly about her
tanned shoulders. "Kevlin? Are you in there?" She shielded her
eyes.

The icy blonde from Tremain's office.

"There you are," she said. Her face flushed. "I came to see
you, if you've got a moment."

"I'm not up to company right now."

Clearly it was Tremain's long hand reaching out to him. He
could guess what the old man wanted to tell him.

"Are you all right?" she asked, adding solicitously, "You look
terrible."

"Thanks."

"You really don't remember me?"

"Dead right." *I don't care to, either.*

"I'm..Trudance. You know, True."

Recognition. "*True? My God. Marci's* little sister?" For a
moment, another woman looked at him from the doorway.

Kevlin blinked again. She was thin, almost willowy, with her
sister's long legs. Wide-set blue eyes and generous mouth. So
classically English looking she had to be Australian.

She seemed to withdraw a little, pulling her hands into her
sleeves, little-girl like, and the illusion vanished. Very different
from Marci. Marci was as shy as a pirate.

"Must've been years since I saw you last," Kevlin said apologetically, sitting up straight. "When I was last in Sydney."

"Don't I look any different?" Her eyes grew incredibly wide and sparkly. He got it. She was putting him on.

"You've ...filled out a bit."

"I can't wear the same swimsuits, if that's what you mean."

True used to go around the beach in the bottom part of a two-piece bikini. Topless.

"Now I remember."

Her cheeks flushed. "Anyway...I'm here because of Grandad."

Kevlin's eyebrows rose. His mouth hardened.

"He's really quite sorry. When Morrison settled down, he told us how you brought back the *Kiwi Kubed*.

Her blue eyes glimmered warmly. "You saved our boat!"

"I saved my own skin, too. Let's not forget that."

"Grandad sent me straight off to find you."

Kevlin shrugged, but she wouldn't be put off. "He regrets how he treated you yesterday. So am I."

She chattered nervously. But Kevlin became aware that he wasn't listening to her. He didn't care about Tremain's "message." He tuned her out.

His worries overwhelmed him. Marci was still missing.

His magazine deadline was ticking away. He had, in truth, very little hope for anything more than lip service from Tremain.

"Hello in there?" True frowned. "You look like you went somewhere. Off for a walkabout. Mentally."

He looked up in surprise. "Let's get out of here," he said urgently.

"That might work," True said.

10

BEACHCOMBER FOYLE'S was little more than a drift-wood shack—always a good sign. Hunkered beyond sand dunes on the lee side of the bay, the building was fronted by a wide old-fashioned porch. A sign, swinging in the breezes, announced that the restaurant had been established more than 100 years ago.

Despite the stormy winds and the chop, Kevlin and True had taken the Manly Ferry across the bay. The ride was blustery, wet and rough, but worth it. Foyle's wasn't crowded at this hour. They managed to find a window table overlooking the beach.

Bringing Trudance seemed an especially good idea. He was curious about her. She was from Tremain's boatyard, the very place he was trying to get some information from.

He hadn't eaten all day, and, after the *Kiwi Cubed* misadventure, he was starving.

"Thanks for the invite," True said. She hunched forward, her hands inside her sleeves. She smelled of wind-dried cottons. "I've not had a proper meal all day."

"Doesn't Tremain feed you?"

"Not his responsibility. I'm a big girl now."

He learned that she was an art student at the University of Sydney and didn't live with her grandfather, and that she wanted to be an illustrator of children's books.

"I only work part time," she said. "with granddad's computers. I fill in at the front desk, and around the office as needed. Sort of a Jillaroo of all trades."

When the waiter eventually got around to them, Kevlin ordered a Tooheys beer and she a Marguerita on the rocks.

"You're a sailor, like Marci?" he inquired. She made a small face.

"*Nooo* way. When I was about eight," she related, "Marci took me out in her dinghy. Granddad always kept one around, and Marci used to steal it for her secret sails around the Sydney Heads. You know, she could handle a dinghy before she could drive a car. She was very good—almost witchy good. And she started winning races in all kinds of weather."

True looked out the window at the dancing whitecaps. "One day when it was raw and gusty—not quite like it is today, but almost as bad — she talked me into joining her. I've never liked the water, but she said she needed me—really needed me —and that she couldn't do it without me. I'd never been out in heavy weather before. As soon as we got away from shore, I begged her to stop and turn back—it was too rough—but she laughed and pressed harder. And harder. You know how delicately she loves to drive boats."

"That's our Marci."

"It was lee rail down all the time. Water sloshed over the sides and I bailed water with my bare hands. It was bail one for the boat, barf one for me. When we finally got back, I was wet, cold, sick, and mad as hatters at my rotten older sister."

Her blue eyes narrowed. "I've hated boats ever since."

"Isn't that what you do now? Work with boats?"

"I work on dry land behind a desk." She raised her chin. "I stay away from the water. I only go near the dock when I have to. In very calm weather. I do *not* go out in sailboats."

"I live on a boat and write about boats."

"And practically breathe them, like Granddad." She looked at him, shaking her head disapprovingly. "You two are so alike."

Alike? Kevlin felt the bile rising.

"I know you've had hard times with him," she said. "People around the harbor joke that his bite is worse than his bark."

"No joke. It was a while before I could sit down."

She laughed, and the waiter came by and they both ordered another round of drinks. Despite the blustery weather, the harbor was bathed in an incomparable light; over across the bay, was one of the most beautiful cities in the world.

"Marci told me once she'd like to cruise the South Pacific some day," True said, hesitatingly. "Just following the trade winds. Island to island. No hurries. No racing."

This was a side of Marci he hadn't seen.

"That was when she was done with racers—and their secrets. When she won the big one. True sat back abruptly and looked away, concerned.

She continued: "Marci loved that new racer of hers. She figured if you really want something bad enough, you just have to keep working until you get it. She worked on it at all hours until it was as slippery in the water as a whale's bottom. She would sit for hours polishing the underbody, the rudders and the keel, going through a series of wet sandings on each of them, but just one way: front to back. She did that by hand and then she ran her fingers over them feeling for imperfections. Then she sat for hours polishing them with special polishing compounds. My God, I think she put part of her soul into that lousy boat."

"Did Marci mention anything...?"

"She's bloody closed mouthed. About herself. Her work. Her boat."

"The keel?"

"Oh, that. That was between her and Grandfather. I was kept pretty much out of it."

"And you didn't hear we planned to meet — some port, somewhere during a race stopover?" Her look told him Marci didn't say anything to her. "Well, I was never wildly popular around here." He offered a wane smile.

"Only with Granddad." She tugged at her sleeves, leaning forward. Her blue eyes were wide and twinkling. She was beginning to enjoy herself. "You *really* don't remember, do you?"

"Lemme see. A few years back, I used to tease you about your tan lines."

"What tan lines?"

"That's right," he laughed. "Kinda skinny, too, right?"

She retreated playfully into her oversized shirt, and then glanced downward. "I managed to fill out a bit, don't you think?"

He glanced away for a moment, his thoughts strayed momentarily to tan lines. Or the lack of them.

"Do you know what I think?"

"I can only guess..." But with a clatter of plates, the waiter arrived with the food. His seafood platter was immense, filled with Sydney rock lobster and shrimp. Her steak looked hearty and properly rare — bloody to him. They dug in; she was not a dainty eater. He didn't hold back either.

When they were finished, they sat back, satiated. Outside the window, another storm front was coming through. The winds were rising.

"Maybe we should talk now," she said.

"OK. What does he want?"

"He wants to see you. At his office."

She sensed his hesitancy. "I think you should go, Kevlin."

The old anger surged back. "I like it better when you're not Tremain's good-will flunky. Why would I want to see *him*?"

Her eyes flared for a moment. "For starters, you bloody well owe me."

"What for?"

"I was the one who got you on the Kiwi boat. When our boat-yard worker got sick, I decided you needed to get a break."

"I almost got one!"

"Granddad blames himself for that accident," she said firmly. "It was his boatyard that put on the rudder."

He fought back his anger, wondering if it was worth a try. There was a lot at stake. He wanted to find Marci. And the dead-lines were pressing relentlessly. Old Tremain was the key.

"I'm trying to help you," True continued, her voice growing tense. "We lost track of Marci just before the storm hit."

"Think the boat sank?"

"Doubt it. *Swagwoman* was built like a tank. She wouldn't sink so quickly Marci couldn't get on the radio or turn on her EPIRB. We'd know."

She shook her head. "There's something else. I overheard her and Grandfather arguing on the radio. The storm was coming. He wanted her to reef down and come in, but she wouldn't hear of it. We think she just snapped off her electronics. End of conversation."

"She must have been flying out there."

"Like a wild thing. But now we don't really know where she is. That boat could cover a lot of territory with Marci at the helm. Out past the Heads, take a hard right on the Tasman Sea, and you're in the Roaring Forties. Dead ahead: Antarctica."

"That's where the old-time clipper ships made their time, with all that wind bowling around the world unobstructed—a deadly place to sail. Even for a racer."

"One other thing: A few hours ago, a search and rescue helicopter came back in. It had infrared radiation equipment on board."

"Infrared? So if there was a little heat on the water's surface...

"...they could tell. Like someone on a boat. Or a life raft."

"Something show up?"

"Not a trace." She looked away, suddenly. "Grandfather thinks that was our last good chance. To locate her. Alive—or not."

Damn. Kevlin's rotten feeling came back. He'd just gotten off *Jolly Swagwoman's* sister ship, *Kiwi Kubed.* Also reportedly built like a battle tank.

Yet one was missing and the other had nearly gone under.

"You hear anything about *Kiwi?* One minute we had steering — then nothing."

"You should have seen Grandfather. He hauled her out with his big crane and ran over to check the new rudders. I saw them, too."

Kevlin leaned forward expectantly. "And?"

"The rudders broke just below the waterline."

"In the carbon fiber lay-up? Or the rudder posts?"

"The fiber." She nodded, equally puzzled. "And in exactly the same places."

"What? I thought we had hit something in the water. One of those overboard steel containers. Maybe even a humpback whale."

His voice trailed off. It was difficult to believe that the carbon composite could crack the way this did. Especially from a noted boat builder.

"Granddad was furious," True said. "I've never seen him that angry." True narrowed her eyes. "*His* rudders don't break, do you understand? Not on his boats."

Something was wrong. Her eyes flared with fear. She abruptly turned away from him to look out past the Heads, where the steep waters of the Tasman Sea roared.

The answer lay out there, somewhere, maybe in the deep.

11

THE FERRY RIDE back to Sydney was rough, with hard whitecaps thrashing around. The wind was a constant low groan: the storm wasn't calming — it was growing worse.

At his side, True held her head down, hands on her stomach.

"You okay?" Kevlin inquired.

"Mm...this ride."

"Take deep breaths. Fix your eyes on a stationery point on the horizon," Kevlin said. "And let's go outside for some fresh air."

True moaned but made her way to the rail. The bouncing was too much and she became seasick.

"Take it easy. You'll get better now."

"Ugh. Ever get seasick?"

"Yeah. From time to time."

"What do you do about it?"

"Nothing much. I remember the advice of Lord Admiral Nelson, who said, "You'll feel better if you sit under a tree.""

"Big comfort. No more boats for me, even harbor ferries," True vowed. She huddled, legs curled under her, on a bench. Her color was returning.

Kevlin turned away, looking back at the Tasman Sea. Marci was out there, somewhere. Ticking away in the back of his mind was his magazine deadline. He was just about past due.

Somehow, he had to turn events around. The first stage was the one he dreaded.

*   *   *

At the Great Barrier Reef Boatyard, they found the old boat builder hunched over the radio dials, switching from chatter to chatter on the ham band radios and then the single sideband radios.

Tremain straightened up. There was an awkward moment's pause.

True eyed the old man carefully: "Grandfather, what is it?"

"We have official notification."

True's mouth hardened.

"Search and rescue concluded their grid. The air search is over."

"They should go out again," Kevlin said.

"I've tried an appeal." He shook his head, sadly. "Nothing works. They have other rescues to make in this storm."

Kevlin asked, "What makes you think that *Swagwoman's* still afloat?"

"Because I *built* her." Whitman bristled.

"You also designed those rudders."

"*Jolly Swagwoman* has floatation bulkheads," Tremain said, exhaling slowly.

"Required by race regulations. Two of them."

"She had *six!* Tremain's eyes glittered with momentary triumph. "She won't sink. Hear me! She's out there somewhere. And Marci is with her."

Kevlin looked away, wishing he could share Tremain's fanaticism. The old man might be right about the boat remaining afloat.

But what about Marci? In those cold waters, time was against her.

*   *   *

"*Whitman.* Do you read me?" the radio crackled.

Startled, Tremain hoisted his bulk close to the microphone. "Loud and clear."

It was the voice of Sydney Search and Rescue.

"Whitman, we have a report from the down-bound Hong Kong freighter *Moshe Maru.* She sighted an overturned vessel.

"Our boat?"

"*Maru* circled the hull, but couldn't get close. The seas are too high. The hull is partially submerged in the water. They couldn't make out a name. We're sending our big chopper out for a quick look-see—the wreck is barely in range."

Tremain spoke quickly. "We can identify the boat."

"Spot on. I was hoping to get a volunteer."

12

R AW GUSTS swayed the big chopper. Below, the black sea was aglitter with whitecaps.

"Did the freighter give you exact coordinates?" Kevlin yelled to the nearest crew member. The helicopter's bumpy ride was making him airsick.

"Yes, sir," Corporal Barry said. "Captain Durstan has them programmed in our flight computer. It's linked to our GPS." He pulled a chocolate bar out of his flight jacket and began eating it. Kevlin's stomach lurched.

"Before the *Moshe Maru* left," Barry shouted between mouthfuls, "they tossed in a couple of EPIRB markers and some yellow sea dye."

"So we ought to find it, no sweat."

"No problem. Between the global positioning system and the markers, we can't miss."

"Anyone else in the vicinity."

"A container ship is diverting her course."

"How close is she?"

"Won't arrive until before dawn. Maybe later."

"Wind seems to be picking up."

"Yeah. Even with reserve fuel, we'll just be able to make it. Our latest weather update says that a new low is dropping down from New Guinea. Rain. Winds gusting to 82 mph."

Hurricane force winds. Kevlin slumped in the cargo area, feeling tightness in his throat. Beside him, the old boat builder clasped and unclasped his hands, deep in thought. Trudance clutched her stomach, white faced.

"I wanted to come," she said grimly. "But I didn't think it'd be like this."

In rough weather, a helicopter flight is much like a boat ride, lurching sideways and up and down motion. It must have taken a great deal of courage for her to make this flight, even if she had known fully what it would be like.

"Well, I'm glad you're here," Kevlin said. True brightened a little, leaning toward him.

*   *   *

A dark sky, with black clouds, glowered over a bilious yellow streak of a horizon, the last light of the day. The helicopter had its searchlights on, illuminating the black, roiling waters. Whitecaps flashed in the gloom.

"Dead ahead, at 12 o'clock!" Captain Durstan was on the intercom. "There's dye and the markers. And something low in the water."

The chopper began dropping out of the sky, swinging from side to side in the wind blasts. Its searchlight flashed on the hull.

"She's overturned," True cried.

Marci's boat lay partly submerged, dead and alone in the water.

"What happened to her keel?" Kevlin was stunned.

The racer's keel should have projected skyward like a sail. All that was left was a jagged stump about a foot above the hull. Nothing remained of the dual rudders.

Corporal Barry wrestled open the chopper's door. The wind roared in, with flecks of sea foam. He leaned out, one hand sheltering his eyes. "No one on board that I can make out," he said.

The chopper settled a bit lower, rocking back and forth as Captain Durstan tried to hover in the high winds.

The searchlight flung its beam wildly in the chop.

"No sign." He shook his head. Far underneath, the hull was hard to see. The shadowy waters conspired to hide the lone boat.

"Sir. I have to ask this for the record. Can you identify this as your boat?" Captain Durstan's voice broke in on the intercom.

"Affirmative," Tremain said slowly. "Our hull all right."

"Then we have visual confirmation. I'll radio Sydney Air-Sea that the hull of *Jolly Swagwoman* has been positively identified."

"Sir, for our report. What do you observe happened?" Corporal Barry had a logbook in hand, approaching the old boat builder.

"The keel is broken off." Tremain said. The ballast bulb is gone. He had a queasy look on his face. "Broken! My God, all that ballast dropped at once...." His brow furrowed, his hands trembled.

"What about Marci?" True spoke haltingly.

"She may have been yanked underwater with the capsizing hull. Or thrown overboard." Tremain uneasily cleared his throat.

"Is there a possibility, just a possibility, that my sister's still down there?" Trudance faced him.

"Trapped under the hull? I want to believe that, too." But he shook his head.

"Sydney reports their receipt of our message." Captain Durstan burst in. "They asked if we had taken shots for the record."

Corporal Barry jumped. "Yes, sir!" In the excitement, he had forgotten.

He quickly located the helicopter's camera and began shooting frame after frame. The pilot moved the chopper about to view all angles.

Below, the hull drifted, a battered relic scoured and beaten by dark waves.

"Hellish thing," Corporal Barry said. "But we've got our shots. I'll advise the captain. We can get back to base."

"Please wait." True interrupted tearfully. "Listen to me. My sister may still be down there."

"A possibility," Tremain said. "If remote."

"It's a chance." Kevlin's eyes were hard. "I need to know for certain."

"What?" Corporal Barry paused, his waiting hand on his mike.

"Just get me in," Kevlin snapped. "Close as you can."

Captain Durstan's voice burst in on the intercom: "What's going on? Close the door."

"Captain," Kevlin shouted. "I'm going on board."

"The hell you are. We ate up most of our fuel getting out here."

"I'll just duck under—for a quick look around."

"A ship's on its way."

"Not much they can do. Look, there may be a woman submerged under that hull. Minutes may count. Do you have underwater gear on board?"

"Just a mask and flippers."

"That'll do. We're wasting time."

"And *fuel*."

"Bloody hell," Captain Durstan swore. "Listen. I am a great fan of Marci's..."

"Then do it."

"This is a military flight," the captain said, making his decision. "But if a civilian...just happens to stand too close to the open hatchway... and happens to fall overboard..."

"Just get me in." Kevlin perspired heavily as he donned the gear, adding a heavy wool sweater and an underwater flashlight. He glanced at the rescue harness in the corner. He'd get hoisted back with the chopper's winch. With Marci.

He wished he felt as boldly as he acted.

"One more thing." Corporal Barry produced a small knife with a red handle.

"Thanks." Kevlin moved to the hatch door. The storm spray coated his face. The great animal was alive and writhing down there. Where he was going was darkness.

Deep into his private fears.

*   *   *

The chopper jockeyed for position, swaying precariously in the growing winds.

"How quick can you make it?" Captain Durstan again.

"In and out. Two minutes."

"No longer. The fuel. Critical. Can't wait!"

Durstan dropped the helicopter to twelve feet above the chop. A wave reared skyward, wetting the bottoms of the wheels. The searchlight beamed down eerily.

"Go dead into the wind. Get as close to the lee side as you can," Kevlin ordered. "I want the windward side of the hull to take those breakers."

At the open door, he hung by a handhold in space, his eyes on the surging black waves below.

He glanced backward: True was white-faced with fear.

"We have to know." Kevlin slipped on his mask. "Either way."

And jumped.

*   *   *

They saw him hit the water and turn for a moment to wave his hand back to them.

A wave rolled over the hull.

When it cleared, he was gone.

13

H E FOUGHT his way downward, the single beam of his flashlight piercing the dark water only a few feet ahead of him. He passed under the cockpit with its tangle of lines winding down.

It was a nightmare. Everything was upside down and dangling. Stainless steel lifelines snaked about. The mast was gone; shredded sails billowed downward in the waves. Above him loomed the open hatchway, its cover torn off. The broken coach roof, with strands of carbon fiber bending in the surge, attested to the violence of the roll

Swallowing hard, he swam into total darkness to resurface in the cabin. Trapped under the hull, there'd be a stale pocket of atmosphere.

A moment of truth. He could delay it no longer.

He gulped air.

It was foul and smelled of bilge bottom. But he was grateful.

The terrible stench he feared was not present.

Breathing heavily, he scanned the upturned hull above him and saw it was still intact. It felt as if he were in a coffin. Cold as the grave.

Inches above his head, waves hissed and surged over the upturned bottom. He shone his light to the left and right: the pocket extended for only a short distance, that of the deepest part of the hull. He could make out floating objects, a life preserver, books, a wooden oar, and plastic food packets. And some clothing.

"Marci?" he yelled. "Are you here?" He banged his fist on a bulkhead repeatedly. "Marci!"

Only echoes came back to him. The small voice in the back of his head drove him on. *He had to know.*

He gulped another breath, then dove.

It was an eerie search, as if he were in another, upside down world—along the forward berth, the stores area, as far as the forward bulkhead with its sealed compartment. He didn't open it for fear of losing buoyancy and sinking the vessel.

She wouldn't be there. No time. It must have been over in seconds. He banged his knife against the bulkhead anyway.

No answer; he expected none. He surfaced again, took several panting breaths, and then began the long search aft. He went over the navigator's station, the galley area, and the rearward pilot berth—the one Marci used at sea.

Nothing.

He scanned the area with his flashlight. No sign of a body. Where was she?

The cold began to work its way through him, piercing his organs. How long had he been under?

The deadline was two minutes.

He glanced at his watch and gasped involuntarily, nearly choking on bilge water. The luminous dial was just crossing the *five*. He had lost track of time.

*   *   *

Hurry. He took another deep breath, then plunged underwater, rushing back down to the cockpit.

His beam of light illuminated the area a few feet at a time. He saw the steering wheel, the winches, and the tangles of lines. Behind them was the inflatable life raft, still intact in its canister.

Unused. A bad sign.

Marci wasn't on board the boat. She hadn't used her inflatable. There were no other choices.

Then he saw it. Unmistakable. A wide band of yellow nylon that snaked down into the water below the cockpit.

Marci's safety harness.

His flashlight beam couldn't illuminate the end. He reached forward to test the harness line.

He yanked and far below, something heavy shifted.

14

H E CAME UP from the deep, gasping for air. A long roller surged over the hull, dousing him; salt spray bit into his eyes. He sputtered, rolled about, searching the skies above him desperately.

But there was only the savage blackness of the night and the sea. He was alone.

Exhausted and shaken, he slumped in the water alongside the hull, letting the waves swirl him about. There was nowhere else to go.

The chopper had left. He'd been down far too long and they couldn't wait.

* * *

Waves boarded the hull, roared over it, cascading down on him as he clung to the side. There was so much foam in the air that it was difficult to breathe, and, this was especially dangerous. His lungs could fill up and he could actually drown from foam.

He started to slip, and then worked his way back. His fingers were numb.

A bad sign. It meant that the cold was getting to him. The water was frigid, but not instantly paralyzing. Cold plays funny tricks with the human body. The sensation of cold is strong at first, but then it recedes and hides away. It's when you stop shivering that you need to worry.

That thought hit home. Shivering. Numb. Mind wandering.

The first signs of the silent killer — hypothermia.

He held his head up, fighting to stay alert and focused. If he couldn't find warmth he would die. He looked about: The hull, near its highest point, would at least get him out of the heat-robbing water. It would not be a great change, but it would help.

Between waves, he swam to the partly submerged transom,

then clambered on board the hull. Scrabbling stiffly, he crawled upward on his belly to the keel area.

He tried to huddle to one side of the stump, away from the wind and waves. Not a hell of a lot better. But it was out of the water. So long as he could stay above the greedy sea, there was hope.

His breath was short, panting, as if in a parching heat. Someone, somewhere, groaned. It was a sound so full of pain and loneliness, that he ached in sympathy. He felt no less sorry when he realized that it was him.

Another wave overran the hull and he started to slip. He threw his arm out, grabbed the keel to keep himself from falling off.

"Shit!" he yelled and yanked his hand back.

The salt water burned his sliced fingers. There was blood, a lot of it. He started to hold up his maimed appendage to see the damage, but that sent him sliding down, down into the clutching waters.

He groped again for anything to hold onto, even the razored keel. But his torn hand wouldn't close. He was losing muscular control.

The awaiting sea couldn't be held off for very much longer. His circumstances were nightmarish. Cold, growing hypothermic — there was no question now.

It was just a matter of time.

* * *

There is heaviness in his lungs. He keeps coughing, but they are filling up from the foam and they are full of pain. He retches seawater.

Out of nowhere, a black wave, huge and cresting, avalanches into the hull, slamming down on him. Its vast weight buries him underwater.

When it finally slashes past, the low, dark shape of the overturned boat fights its way back to the surface and pops free.

Alone.

15

LIGHTNING RIPPED through dark skies. A sudden wind shift sent the speeding helicopter lurching sideways.

Corporal Barry had to roar to make himself heard above the noise of the wind, rotors and laboring engine.

Tremain was not about to be silenced. "What about the man you've left down there?"

Barry worked his way across the bouncing cabin to shove a life preserver at Tremain, pushing him down in his seat. "He waited too long. Bad luck, but we got our own problems now."

Barry grabbed for a handhold, struggling to stay upright. "The wind's switched. It's come between us and the land."

True clutched at her stomach as she looked out the window at the waves below. A lightning flash illuminated huge, roiling waters capped with white, reaching hungrily toward the sky. She shivered.

"She's trying to blow us out to sea."

Tremain cocked a wary eye at the airman. "You mean, the storm? Make sense, man."

"The *Lady*," Barry laughed uneasily. "I call her the Lady."

"Get hold of yourself."

Barry's eyes turned haunted. "I've been here before. We were pulling survivors off the *Paladarn*—and I saw her. Just for a second."

"Who'd you see?" True was wary now.

"The *Lady*. I saw a gray lady in the night."

"The storm?"

"I wasn't supposed to see," the young airman continued. "But I saw her *face*. That meant something."

"Superstitious nonsense. It's just a storm," Tremain said, shaking his head. "A bad one. But just a storm."

"It's more."

"Like what?"

"Look out there." Barry hesitated momentarily.

A shudder ran through the helicopter as it fought its way through a wind blast.

"S*he's come back. For me.*"

"Don't be a superstitious fool."

"Hear her?" Barry yelled, cocking his head to listen better. "Wind's heading us. We've got almost no speed at all." There was terror in Barry's voice.

True turned from the window, her face white. "But we can reach land...?"

Barry looked away.

Tremain said harshly, "Corporal Barry, we have enough fuel, don't we?

"Don't we?"

They could barely hear the answer. It came in a low, dark voice.

"No."

16

BY DAWN, the New Zealand container ship *Fitzworth Imperial* was plowing through vast mountains of water. The seas were huge, surging forward like walls, making even the large steel cargo ship bounce around.

Captain Bruce Whitsday checked the GPS readout and ordered slow ahead. Beneath him, he could feel the rumble lessen and the hull moved easier. He shook his head. There was no doubt. This was the position they had been given. The exact coordinates.

Where was it? He grabbed a pair of high-powered binoculars and stepped outside on the bridge deck. A blast of wind hit him; he braced himself on the rail, and scanned the seas. Again.

There it was. Lying lifeless in the water. A thing forlorn.

"Contact," he yelled, pointing. "Fifteen degrees off the starboard bow."

If he had not had the exact global positioning coordinates, he would have missed the hulk entirely. Slowly, the massive ship fought her way toward the hulk.

"No one aboard, captain." It was the first mate.

Another wave overran *Jolly Swagwoman*, inundating her low lying hull with green water and foam.

They both began their visual search as the wheelsman tried to maintain their position. They scanned the nearby waters methodically for a yellow life raft or a body in a life jacket.

"Any luck?" It was Captain Whitsby.

"No." The mate shook his head. "And frankly, I don't see how anyone could have survived."

"Have Sparks send this message to Sydney's Search and Rescue: We have located the wreck, are alongside, and observe no survivors."

"Will do, Captain."

"Tell Mr. Hidary: he can have a go at it, if he's ready."

The first mate thumbed the button on the intercom; minutes later, a small, wiry man entered the bridge. He was dressed in black neoprene rubber from head to toe; in one sinewy arm he carried SCUBA gear, and, in the other, heavy swim fins and a diving mask. Strapped onto his leg was a diving knife.

"I can't order you to go," the Captain said.

"We need to find out, don't we?"

"Just pop below for a quick look. Then get the hell back. We'll have enough trouble retrieving you in these seas."

*   *   *

Timing his entry to the motion of the ship, the diver grunted as he dropped off. The cold, green water enveloped him.

He gave the overturned hull a wide berth, swimming slowly around, looking for any clues to the accident. Tangles of lines and rigging hung downward, fading into green darkness. He could make out a stub of a mast, twisted and bent.

Turning on his diving light, he submerged deep under the boat, finding his way to the overturned cockpit. There was motion here; the hull was bouncing up and down. He'd have to be careful. Inside the storm-shaken confines, he could get hit on the head or cut himself on the jagged, broken edges. Or tangled in the black, snaking lines of rigging.

An upside down wheel, drifting aimlessly, was steered by the empty seas.

He sucked a sharp breath of air, his SCUBA squeaking. Time to enter the upside down cabin. The yawing void. And perhaps, find the final truth.

He moved forward, shining his light, debris bobbing in his wake all the way to the watertight bulkhead. Then back toward the aft section.

Nothing.

He didn't expect anything, but the formal examination had to be done. The details of the tragedy reported.

He moved upward toward the bilge, testing. At the top, he found a large air bubble that had been trapped inside when the hull overturned.

Reluctantly, he slipped back his diving mask to sniff the air, ready to put it back on if the atmosphere was foul.

He sniffed, tentatively. A smell of rotting stores. Musky, but not unendurable.

"Anyone here?" He called out. His voice echoed eerily inside the air chamber. He shone his light about.

He turned to leave.

Out of the darkness, a voice rasped back at him:

"Not so damned loud."

*   *   *

He blinked, shivering uncontrollably, and rubbed salt water from his eyes. His body ached from the pounding; his hands were raw, bleeding. In the bright lights, his eyes barely focused.

He was in a small, white room, and judging from the disturbing motion, aboard a ship. A big one.

"Well, are we starting to come around?"

It was the ship's captain, pouring a cup of steaming hot tea from a thermos.

"I'm only half drowned," Kevlin mumbled. He was coughing up seawater. But alive.

"How'd you find me?"

"Your friends on the chopper. They radioed the GPS position of the hull and told us you were still with it. We looked, but no one was aboard. "

"Yeah. I figured the hull would float, so I went underneath and built myself a little nest in the air bubble. I tied some floorboards and other stuff together. I was out of the water, mostly. But not the most comfortable way to spend the night."

A bout of shivers caught him again, but he had time to ask: "My friends in the chopper? Can you radio ahead to tell them I'm OK?"

"They...er, changed course, trying to make it in."

A new fear came to Kevlin. "Are you in touch with shore?"

"Yes," the captain said. He hesitated a moment, weighing his options.

Finally he said, "Sorry, but your friends never made it in."

17

THE FISHING BOAT'S BOW lunged up and down in the heavy waves, its heavy anchor wedged in the helicopter's aluminum fuselage. Creaking and groaning, the hook was slowly tearing the silvery bird apart.

Just inside the twisted doorway, fisherman Brad Trushaw braced himself against a wave's lurch. "Damnation," he swore, squinting his eyes for a better look.

Already the helicopter's cabin was knee-deep in surging water, overflowing his fisherman's boots. *Where were they? Were they still alive?*

He had gotten their radio message and their GPS coordinates. His boat was nearest and he responded. He had seen the chopper barely afloat and speared it through the open hatchway with his fisherman's anchor.

He shivered, gritting his teeth. The whole bloody thing could go at any time.

"Help... them!"

From the corner of the cabin, a man in a corporal's uniform nodded weakly toward the other passengers still belted to their seats. Trushaw saw a young blonde woman and a battered, white haired older man.

"We'll get you all out," Trushaw said, bravely as he could manage. "Who's in charge?"

"Barry," came the weak voice. "...all here. Captain's forward."

Trushaw moved to the cockpit, glancing in. It was partly submerged and he could see a helmeted head slowly bobbing face down in the murky waters. He was gone.

He returned to the chopper's cabin, making his decision. "You go first, ma'am," Trushaw said, slipping forward to unsnap the woman's seat harness. But there was no response: her head lay to one side, eyes closed and face a chalky white. Two gone?

A shudder ran through the fragile craft; a wave splashed through the broken windows. The water grew higher as the bird tilted further forward.

"Hurry, sir" urged Corporal Barry. "Not much time left."

Trushaw wrestled the woman's limp form to the door, splashing through the water. He yelled up to the ship's bridge. "First one's coming out."

A heavy rope lowered over the ship's bow. In the pitching of the partly submerged helicopter, it was difficult to catch.

He lunged once, twice.

On the third attempt, he grabbed the line through the doorway and spun it around the woman's waist. He tied a secure bowline knot.

"Hoist away!" he yelled; moments later, she was airborne and over the railing aboard the boat.

Trushaw waited for the hawser to return, and, clutching it under one arm, waded forward. The water had grown deeper. Three men were left. One was dead, one dying, and one in shock. His priority now was to the man who was conscious and looking at him.

"Can you help?" Trushaw tried to get Barry moving. "Unhitch yourself?" His flight seat was partly underwater.

Barry feebly waved him off. "Get them first," Barry muttered. "The civilians."

"We'll get you all out," Trushaw tried to reassure the corporal. "How about you next?"

"We're Search and Rescue. We leave last."

Trushaw was in no mood to argue. Under his feet, he felt the buoyancy slipping away; the angle was increasing.

"Just give us a hand," Trushaw shot at Barry, but the young Corporal made no move to unsnap himself. Transfixed, his eyes seemed to be locked on some hidden horror outside the wreck.

He'll wait, Trushaw decided.

He turned to the old man, his face fallen forward and was almost in the water, barely held upright by his floatation device and his harness. A few more inches of water in the cabin and he'd be gone.

The rescuer hefted his bulk against the heavy older man,

unsnapping his seat harness and muscling him out of the seat. In the deepening water, he wrestled him toward the open hatchway. Once again, he tied a bowline under his arms.

"Haul away," he yelled, and the man disappeared above him, reeled up to the pitching bow.

Two down — one to go.

The craft lurched again.

"I'm coming..." Trushaw yelled, desperately splashing forward, rope in hand.

"The Lady." He heard the young corporal exclaim in a low, hoarse voice. *"You're here."*

It was a voice filled with awe, and not a little fear. Clearly, he saw something. His eyes grew wide.

He smiled as if, at last, to welcome something.

*   *   *

A mountain of water avalanched into the helicopter, shooting it upward, then slamming it down. Waves exploded across the craft, making it pitch and roll, then twist violently on its side.

Cold sliced into them. The shock hit like death itself.

Spray blinded Trushaw, waist deep in water, still hanging onto the rope.

Suddenly, he felt himself yanked backward, out of the chopper's doorway, and dangling in the wind.

He blinked his eyes. Below him were only black waves.

The chopper was gone, along with the corporal, swallowed in the spray, as if they had never been.

18

THE SEASIDE CHAPEL rang its bells slowly, one bell
mourning each year of the young sailor's lost life. The pews
in the dim light were filled with mourners; many stood in the rear
vestibule, their heads bowed during the traditional memorial service to those lost at sea.

"For those of us who remain," the minister intoned, "we have
the shining example of Marcia Whitman."

Kevlin squirmed uneasily in the church pew, unable to get any
comfort from the minister's words.

"Her dream was to follow the way of the sea and the wind,"
the minister continued. "She died doing that which she loved. She
lived a sailor and she died a sailor. May she rest in peace beneath
the waves."

As the seaman's choir began singing "Abide with me," Kevlin
glanced out the window. Specters of clouds were ghosting overhead.

Between the patches of gray, weak sunlight filtered through,
golden rays beaming down on the churchyard's tombstones of
sailors, a small cluster of wooden, limestone and granite markers.

She would never rest among them. The service was only a
memorial. There was no coffin. No body to lie at rest. No closure.

Lost at sea. Forever. His head sunk on his chest, his eyes
watering.

He knew why.

He glanced to the mourners to either side of him, then closed
his eyes and looked downward. This was the hard part, trying not
to remember.

He couldn't help himself. He tried to visualize her at the helm
of her beloved racing boat, every sail fully charged, lunging and

rushing through the waves. So vibrant, so alive.

He tried to fill his mind with her image.

Outside, the wind pressed hard against the stained glass windows, rattling them. He wiped his perspiring brow. It wasn't working.

Behind him there was a slight flurry of activity. Someone was entering the pew. He turned: It was Tremain and True.

Tremain whispered: "We thought you had left."

"Had to stay on." Kevlin shook his head, clearing his thoughts. "Just a few more days.

He had not seen them since the helicopter ride out to the overturned boat, though he'd managed to talk to them by telephone briefly in the hospital. Tremain had a bandaged right hand, held in a shoulder brace. True had several cuts on her face, revealed when her blonde hair fell to one side.

"I'm so sorry..." Kevlin began, but True abruptly leaned back in her pew.

"If only we could have her back."

The old man shook his head sadly. The choir began another hymn, and Kevlin tried to follow the old, familiar words.

In the distance, the wind had a primeval sound. Out past the headlands, the dark seas were wild, untamed.

Something that called to him.

* * *

They were outside the chapel now. Kevlin was aware that Tremain was asking him a question.

"I'll be going soon." He tried to focus on his friends. Actually, they did not know he had to fight to remain here for the funeral services. The magazine wanted him back, as soon as he had fully recovered.

"Did you get your story off?"

Kevlin nodded. "Yeah. But I don't really remember much of what I sent."

Actually, he was thankful he got anything off at all. To their curious looks, he explained: "I got to the ship's communications section — the ship that picked me up out of the water. And sent something back to our C-center."

He didn't mention that he had been shaking from exposure and the cold when he keyboarded his message. What he sent should have been enough to let them change the cover wording to update it and do a sidebar story inside.

In fact, the magazine should be rolling off the presses by now.

True hesitated: "When you were...down there...did you find ...anything?"

He knew what she was asking. He tried to find the right words. "I didn't find...anything. I looked everywhere inside, except the sealed forward compartments. They were still intact. I checked."

"No trace? None at all?"

"No. Her exposure suit was still below. In fact, that probably was what saved me — I managed to put it on when I stayed under the boat, waiting for rescue. I looked around. When I was under the cockpit, the life raft was still intact, in its sealed container. So she didn't deploy it."

They knew what that meant. She was not onboard. Her life raft was. No hope of survival out there without it.

Kevlin continued: "But out in the cockpit, I did find Marci's safety harness."

Tremain looked up.

"The tether was broken."

Tremain's face fell. "Hard to believe."

Kevlin nodded. The images were coming back. He fought back a rising gorge. His eyes started to tear.

He couldn't tell them.

"Must have taken tremendous forces," Tremain was saying. "It was over quickly, then."

True wiped her eyes. "She didn't suffer?"

"The boat must've flipped over fast. She undoubtedly was flung overboard..."

True looked searchingly at Kevlin "What is it, Kevlin?"

A shiver went through him. Kevlin turned away, his instincts roaring, beginning to remember what he wanted so desperately to forget.

*   *   *

Once again, he hung in the dark depths below the broken sailboat's cockpit, the roil of the storm waves above him. Beneath him hung a yellow nylon line, lit by the dying rays of his flashlight.

There was something odd about the way it hung.

It didn't twist back and forth in the current; it dragged, pointing straight down to infinity.

Something weighted it down.

Blood pounding in his head, he descended into the dark, hand over hand, his lungs bursting. In the feeble rays of his light, deeper in the depths, he could make out the flicker of something bright.

Short blonde hair, swirling wraith-like in the water.

He turned away before he could see more. She'd been down there...for days.

He hung there, lungs bursting.

He couldn't bring her up. Not *now.*

With trembling hand, his knife slashed at the yellow line. He could only watch for a moment as what remained slid into the dark, waiting depths.

A sailor's death.

"Farewell, my love," he whispered.

He barely made it back to the surface.

*   *   *

He suddenly realized that mourners were staring at him. Stumbling, he fled wordlessly past True and the others.

Tears blurred his vision as he ran from the old chapel toward the awaiting ocean.

Alone he faced the dark sea, clenching his fists.

Out there lay something that would not let him rest.

19

THE HARBOR LIGHT was still a gray veil in the east when someone lifted the cabin hatch above him. Light and wind flickered in, and with it, a piece of paper that floated down with Bruce's voice. "Text message. For you. Somebody from the boat-yard came over with it."

Kevlin grabbed the paper and groaned, his muscles stiff from his underwater ordeal. The pain came from every part of his body. Bruce's face appeared in the hatch opening, grinning lopsidedly. "How are we today?"

"Don't know about you, but I'm OK." Kevlin rubbed his eyes..

"Well, you are definitely among the living. You were talking in your sleep. About the keel on Marci's boat."

"Yeah. It was a sharp break. I saw that first hand. A real sharp break." He held up his bandaged hand.

"Just a stump sticking up. Nothing."

"I don't know. Something odd...I haven't put it together yet."

Bruce's grin grew more lop-sided. "I gotta check something."

Kevlin grew tense. " What've you got, Brucey?"

"Later. Cheerio." And Bruce was gone.

Odd. He unfolded the message from Sam at *Megasail*. No doubt this would be Sam's congratulations on his exclusive update. The one he had filed onboard the ship, after they rescued him.

A lot of agony. But now, a ray of sunshine. A little begrudging appreciation for his hard work.

Probably telling him to stay on a few more days until he recovered. Felt better. Stuff like that. Yeah, maybe.

Printed on crumpled paper were the words, "Your employment with this magazine is hereby terminated."

He stopped smiling.

20

BEHIND HIS DESK in the boatyard office, still partly wrapped in a shoulder bandage after his release from the hospital, Tremain diplomatically avoided Kevlin's angry gaze. True flashed him a wan, but understanding smile.

It was obvious that both had read Sam's fax when it came off the machine. In all probability, so had everyone in the entire goddam boatyard office. There was nothing private about a text message. Sam had known that!

Kevlin's face flushed. He was getting the business. Now he was a magazine journalist without a magazine. Stranded in Sydney.

"The boss blows hot and cold." Kevlin tried to shrug and make light of it, but he had no illusions on how precarious his position was.

"I don't give a rat's rosy rear end about the magazine," Tremain snorted, "I told you that up front."

Kevlin gritted his teeth and said nothing.

"Going to stop mucking about?" Tremain seemed pleased. The quality of mercy was in short supply today in the boatyard.

"Not bloody likely!"

"You're out of a job."

Kevlin looked over at True, whose face was turning a faint pink. It was turning out to be a miserable day all around. His bandaged hand was beginning to ache again.

He drew himself upright. "It's only over when I fall down, don't move any more, and they drive a stake through my heart."

He softened his tone. "In the meantime, I need one more thing."

"A bloody miracle?"

"Your keel."

Tremain's face began to glow red.

"The public has never seen it."

"Never will," Tremain began to bellow. "It's bloody well 4,000 feet under the bloody Tasman Sea."

"I mean your *design*."

Tremain stopped short. "That's secret."

True stepped forward, facing Tremain. "But it's gone with Marci, isn't it, Granddad?"

"I don't even like to think about it."

"Time to talk," True pursued softly. "You can't shoulder all the blame forever."

"I assume all responsibility for the design. Always have."

"Marci had a big role in the development of that keel, Grandfather. Change after change. She kept after everyone to redesign it—make it sleeker, longer and deeper.."

"I OK'd the design. "I'm the bloke who's responsible."

"She paid a terrible price."

"If I had told her no, she might still be alive today. She wouldn't have had to go out there for sea trials so late."

"What's this?" Kevlin sensed something new.

Tremain looked hard at Kevlin. "None of your damned business."

True said, "They were late on the design and getting the boat ready."

"So that's why she was out there when she was...during the storm."

"Storms happen," Tremain snarled. "Couldn't predict that."

"But she was so close to the deadline," Kevlin said. "She had to drive her boat to get in the required qualifying run."

True said, "She could have backed off."

"No, not Marci." It was all coming out now.

Tremain looked anguished. "She had to qualify...and she had to have her own sea trials at the same time. Had to do both at once, then bring the boat back to the yard for any refits and final tune up. We were late."

The old man turned away, hiding his face. "Late on the design. Late in getting the boat fitted out. Late for sea trials. I was responsible...for everything." He turned away.

"And she would not give up and come back in. Even in the storm."

There was a moment of silence. True pressed a hand to Tremain's shoulder. "It's over, Grandfather—all over. And time to get it behind us."

It was becoming clear to Kevlin that True was changing. She was saying her mind and expressing herself. And that her grandfather was, maybe at last, listening to her.

Tremain sighed deeply. "I can't."

True emphasized: "Time to get on with it. My sister would want that."

Tremain straightened up and nodded.

"Look at me, Grandfather. Am I right?"

Something seemed to relax a bit inside the old boatbuilder. But that lasted only a moment.

With a growl, Tremain turned to Kevlin. "You're lucky."

"What?"

"Turns out I'm in a merciful mood today. Yes, you're damned lucky."

True permitted herself a small smile. It was clear to Kevlin whose side she was on.

Tremain caught the look. "This isn't because of my granddaughter over there. Don't think I'm being led around by the nose."

'No Sir."

"It's just too late for our design to aid other racers. By the time the next bloody RAAW rolls around—if there is another one—we'll have something new."

"A keel that doesn't break." Kevlin frowned. "No matter what."

Aargh! The old man flushed angrily. "Never should have happened."

"Like the rudders on the *Kiwi Cubed* shouldn't have busted? Both of them?"

True quickly held up her hands. "Granddad, don't you think it's time to take Kevlin for a little visit?"

"By God, *yes*," Tremain said, rubbing his hands together.

A gleam came to his eyes. "The Skunk Works for Kevlin it is."

21

AT THE BOTTOM of the steel staircase, below the boat-yard, was a dimly lit steel security door, massive in appearance. Tremain slid a plastic card into the computerized lock. A light flashed. The lock hummed and the door swung open to reveal a vault-like room.

Overhead lights flickered on and Tremain spread an arm like a conjurer. "Welcome to the Skunk Works."

So that was it, thought Kevlin. This was the old man's secret research laboratory. Under spotlights, a giant fin rose atop a wooden ramp, black and dangerous looking.

Kevlin said. "The keel,"

"Just our mock-up," Tremain said. "We used this for our casting mold."

"It's so thin!"

"Like a knife blade. That's what helped make *Swagwoman* fast. The keel offers very little resistance to the flow of water around the hull. Most boats have thick keels where they join the hull. We've done away with that."

The bottom was equipped with a flattened tear-drop-shaped torpedo bulb.

Tremain explained: "The actual bulb is cast of depleted uranium—the densest, heaviest material there is. We got ours from a European government source behind what used to be the Iron Curtain. They have links through certain Pacific Rim companies."

Kevlin frowned. "When do we get to the secret stuff?"

True pressed Tremain's arm. "Let him see what you and Marci came up with."

The old boat builder stood stolidly for a moment, grunted, then whisked away a canvas covering. Under the lights shone stainless steel cylinders and levers attached to a huge black bolt.

"So that's it?" Kevlin drew closer.

"Show him how it works. *Go on.*" True urged.

Tremain stepped up to a complex hydraulic system and pumped a short stainless steel lever. The bolt rotated to one side.

"Imagine," Tremain said, "the keel is attached below the cylinder. With a few pumps this cylinder will rotate, moving tons of ballast to one side — up to twenty degrees."

Kevlin nodded, absorbed. "The boat would stop heeling and straighten up."

"Sail harder, sail faster," Tremain emphasized. "Win races."

"Articulated keels are new, but hardly experimental."

"Keep watching," Tremain said, grabbing another set of levers. "This is what makes the keel special."

The massive center bolt slid forward, then backward. "We can position the keel weight wherever in the hull we want it: side to side, forward or backward."

Kevlin leaned forward, impressed.

"With the *double canting* keel, we can perfectly balance the boat to all conditions. We can get up and plane sooner and do it longer than any boat in the race. Carry more sail in heavier winds than any other boat in that race."

"Ingenious!" Kevlin reached for a piece of engineering paper and borrowed a pen. He began to sketch the keel as he talked. Hydrodynamics?"

"Fully tested, in model form," Tremain said. "We had a lab run a computer simulation beforehand. We got superb flow, with minimal resistance."

Kevlin sketched the keel as Tremain continued: "It worked. We had a racer that went like hellfire. The design was superb. Superb!" His eyes shone with excitement.

"I can appreciate that, sir," Kevlin said. "Mind if I see what's on top."

Climbing the wooden frame, he ran his hand along the juncture where the keel joined the hull. He took a deep breath: "Do you think the double canting mechanism was the problem? Why Marci's boat went under?"

"No!" Tremain was adamant. "We had it all calculated. Massive carbon fiber lay-ups. Heavy stainless steel. Everything over engineered."

"Yes, sir, but...."

"No more a chance of that failing than a wing falling off an airplane."

Kevlin ran his hand over the surface. "Maybe something else is at work here. Let me think back."

"What are you getting at?"

He paused, deep in thought. "When I was atop the hull that night, I was about here and my hand was over the top." He moved his hand about. "It felt jagged here ... and smooth there."

Tremain was curious. "Up where?"

"Here. About six inches to a foot beyond the hull juncture."

"Then you're talking about the keel itself. The double-canting mechanism was entirely within the hull."

"I was trying to hang on. My hand got cut as I was washed off."

"On the keel stub."

"Yeah. I remember that in the center of the keel stub, there was a sharp part. But the outside was sort of lumpy, but smooth. Odd."

"Son, that can't be right." Tremain was moving behind him. "That keel was carbon fiber. And carbon fiber breaks rough. It splinters."

"This didn't splinter. "

Tremain frowned, unconvinced.

"Something else. Maybe the outside fibers snapped first. So it hung on by the center section and wore the outside smooth."

True nodded. "Until the center snapped?"

Tremain stepped atop the mold, shaking his head. "Not bloody likely."

*　　*　　*

Kevlin squared his shoulders. "Let's just stop. Pause. Think a bloody moment."

Tremain bored in: "Graphite composite is stronger than steel. That bloody keel could have dropped off a skyscraper—and it still would have survived, the way we designed it."

"Designed it? Okay, but what about the layup?"

Tremain turned to face him, not looking too pleased.

"No," he said with a heavy look. "We didn't actually build the keel. We don't have the machinery."

"Someone else built it?" Kevlin had a pang of fear. He was almost afraid of the answer.

"It was a custom job. Had to be done at a special foundry."

"Let me get this straight. Marci's boat had her custom keel built at an *outside* foundry?"

True started to say something, but Tremain interrupted. "I know what you're thinking and you can just put it out of your mind."

But Kevlin only stared at the keel.

22

IT LAY near the waterfront in a low, concrete block building that reminded Kevlin of a World War II bunker. Sand had drifted part way up the Outback Foundry's massive walls and at one corner, facing the water, was a rusted steel door.

"Let me prepare you a bit," True said, stopping him at the entrance. "Bush is different."

So what else is new? Kevlin glanced warily at the building. In the failing light, it seemed morbid, a dead thing cut from its time. He was more than willing to delay entrance.

"Father's done business with him for ages," True explained. "But you have to understand he's old school. From the Outback."

"Stranger than Brucey?"

"In comparison, Bruce is an epitome of charm and erudition. Bush can hardly spell his own name, but he's a bloody miracle worker with machinery."

"Been in the business for a long time?"

"Years. Remember when the first carbon fiber rudders came out? They were hot with the racing crowd?"

"They saved a lot of weight. But broke all the time."

"The very ones. Well, Bush figured out how the fibers had to run in certain directions to get the strength that you needed for ocean racing. From there he branched into masts and keels."

"That don't usually break."

"You don't last long in this business if they do." True fell silent for a moment, thinking. "Layup manufacture is difficult."

"Not rocket scientist stuff."

"No. It's working with poisonous, stinking chemicals in stifling heat with fumes that can kill you. Grandfather calls it the 'pox.' Short for epoxy."

"Must be fun trying to get people to work with the stuff."

From just inside the office a voice rumbled wearily: "Damned near impossible." It was quickly followed by a hopeful: "You looking for work?"

Hobart "Bush" Marin turned out to be a portly Sydneysider with a bushy silver beard and a wild rat's nest of hair sticking out from under a battered hat. He nodded in their direction, rising from behind a gray steel desk. A large dog with more than a touch of dingo lineage looked momentarily up from its place on the floor.

"Good to see you again, Bush," True said, offering her hand and smiling sweetly. "Grandfather suggested we talk to you."

Bush smiled back, equally full of charm. He chuckled. "No, he didn't."

He turned away, heading deeper into the foundry. Only his voice drifted back to them:

"But I know what you're after. Might as well get this over with. Coming?"

*   *   *

The foundry reeked of high-tech petrochemicals and molten metals.

"This here's our main layup mold." Bush waved his hand to indicate a tall steel chamber. It was a massive structure, but slender—almost delicate in design like a flower. Long lines of black carbon fiber sprung from it like strands in a spider's web.

Kevlin walked carefully up the scaffolding and let his right hand touch several feet below the top. "The break came...here!"

"What?" Bush frowned. His attitude changed. "Are you sure?"

"I was there. On board. See?" Kevlin held up his bandaged hand.

"You're the one?" Bush shook his head.

"I cut it on your keel."

A cloud of worry hung over Bush. "I supervised the layup personally. You know what that means?"

True shook her head.

"No mistakes. Not in the layup. My old mate Tremain's a great boat designer, but he didn't allow for reserve strength."

Kevlin looked hard.

"I always felt that the keel should have been thicker. Not so thin. I begged him: Let me just add a couple more layers of carbon fibre, at least. Maybe....maybe..."

"Out with it," True demanded.

Bush shook his head sadly. "I swear the layup was perfect. If the keel snapped, it was because of the design."

He looked at them, eyes glowing in anger.

"If Marci died because of that—it wasn't me."

23

DARK CLOUDs scudded ominously across a full moon, causing shadows to flit across the waterfront. The wind was full out of the east, blowing sand and dust; from the harbor came the dank smell of salt air.

They had arrived from the back roads of the harbor to find the foundry's parking lot dark. Black, in fact: Bush apparently didn't believe in the extravagance of yard lights. True and Kevlin parked the car, then cautiously moved toward the entry.

"You sure you want to do this?" True asked, nervously.

"We need to have a proper look around," Kevlin said. "Bush wasn't telling us much."

"It's certainly dark enough," True grumbled, turning up the collar of her light jacket. "But there should be some workers here. They're laying up new rudders for the Kiwi boat."

Kevlin shone a flashlight on the door. There was no padlock or other external electronic security measure he could see. He gripped the massive latch; the heavy steel door swung easily opened.

"Hello. We're here." True's voice echoed about.

Inside, a single overhead bulb illuminated Bush's office. The foundry was a dark land of mysteries, cramped with machinery and the dying red glow of blast furnaces, redolent of petrochemicals. Something scurried past, making clicking noises with its claws on the concrete flooring.

"No sign of anyone." Kevlin's flashlight beam flicked over keel molds, charred benches and a pulley for pouring...and then stopped.

Beside the foundry, in the pool of light, lay the body of a man.

"What...?" Kevlin forced himself to move closer, deeper into the furnace's heat.

His arms were thrown wide, as if defending himself. There

was blood on the man's face and puddled about him on the floor, congealing in the heated air. One eye stared in accusation.

Kevlin touched the man's wrist. The only pulse was the gentle rumble of the nearby blast furnace.

Rising, he lurched back to True.

"Who is it?" Her voice was quavering.

His voice was toneless. "Bruce."

24

"MY, GOD," cried True. "What happened to him?" Kevlin held her to one side. "I can't tell: there's blood all over."

"Is he alive?" Her eyes grew wide with fear.

"We should call...." he began. There was a flashing white light in the doorway.

Kevlin wheeled toward it. "Who's there?"

"Police," came the answer.

A uniformed cop came forward, light glinting off his drawn revolver.

"Easy, mate," Kevlin said. "We just got here."

"Yeah, well you set off the entry alarm some time ago." The cop's light glanced on the body, sprawled in blood behind them. "Holy shit!"

"We just found him," Kevlin said. He spread his hands wide, emphasizing his point.

"The lady here... left her...backpack. We came back for it."

The cop shone his light about, then backed up, his face unrecognizable in the light.

"We should call an ambulance," True pleaded.

The revolver was very steady now.

"Don't move," the cop said, his voice low and even.

"The ambulance? I think we should hurry," True added.

"We've got a double homicide," he called into his radio. "Get some backup and then haul your ass in here."

"Double?" Kevlin felt trapped.

"The guy lying over there, asshole."

*　　*　　*

From a dark corner of the parking lot, the man in the shadows inhaled sharply. He saw the second policeman slam the patrol car's door shut, then sprint toward the building. The light was dim, but in the crazily bobbing beam of the cop's flashlight, he could make out the glint of a drawn revolver.

Good. All was falling into place.

It had been a bloody night, and he could not erase the images of what he had done. His mind raced to the eternal question: What does a single death matter when so much is at stake?

In his mind's eye, he formed an image, that of a giant measuring scale, beneath which dangled two chains. On the one side were two human lives, on the other, a multitude.

The balance tilted in favor of the many. Always.

No matter the failings of his conscience, he was justified through mathematics. In the numbers there was reason and truth. And sanity.

Over the howl of the wind arose the sound of angry voices. Arguing.

In the light of the doorway a knot of people emerged.

One was the magazine editor and the other the short blonde. There was the glitter of something on their wrists. Handcuffs.

He waited until the police put them forcibly in the car. The two were in custody, the obvious suspects for the killings. It was enough.

The man in black detached himself from the shadows and began to move quickly along the dark waterfront.

His evening's work was just beginning.

25

T HE LIGHTS of the police cruiser picked out Bruce's mooring slip in harsh contrast, pushing the shadows back to the
fringes of the night.

"OK, you're here," the cop said in an official flat voice.

"Thanks," Kevlin said, equally enthusiastic as he climbed from
the car door and stared down the dock.

He was being released after hours of questioning. It was appar-
ent that he and True had only stumbled upon the double murders.

Still, questions lingered: why had they come back to the
foundry when they did? What had they seen? What had they
done?

The cops were not satisfied, but didn't have enough to hold
them. They'd return with more bouts of questioning—of that
Kevlin had no doubt. They were suspicious. And cops.

"Just don't leave town," the cop grunted and slammed the door.
The cruiser backed rapidly, tossing gravel.

*   *   *

Kevlin began walking down the pier. The boat lay ahead, a low
shadow in a dark harbor, its black masts driving spikes into the
moon, raking the silvery clouds.

The harbor wind was chill at this hour; Kevlin shivered. His
cold berth in the forepeak awaited.

The cabin was silent except for the movement of the old boat.
Its masts creaked in the harbor breezes, the rigging humming
softly.

He searched for a flashlight, fumbling along in the dark, then
lifted his head. Something else.

There, in the night, he heard it.

A scratching noise. It came from the forward area, near his berth.

There. It came again. Distinctly. Faint, a rustling sound, as if papers being moved.

The cold metal of the ship's flashlight filled his hand. It was a solid, confident weight, enough to be used as a weapon.

Cat-like, he crept forward toward the sound of the intruder. After a night of frustrations, he'd have some action. And maybe some answers. His heart pounded.

"Let's find out who you are," he snarled under his breath.

At the bulkhead, he put his ear to the door. The only sound to break the darkness was his own breathing.

He placed his hand on the door's cold steel and pushed it open. His muscles tensed.

Silence. Blackness.

And a faint odor.

The bitter tang of fear, filling the hold.

His instincts screamed a warning. He started to spin away.

Far too slowly.

26

SOFT LIGHTS filled the air about him, sending gentle shadows flickering. He put his hands to his head and felt rough cloth, and below it, pain. Bandages. Something had happened to him.

Out of the corner of his eye, he saw her. She was slumped in the Captain's chair, pulled up close to his berth. Her blonde hair fell softly about her face, her long legs drawn nearly up to her chin.

Marci. She had come back to him.

Tears stung his eyes and he tried to speak, but the shadows merged. Darkness swallowed him again.

*   *   *

The rosy glow of daybreak seeped into the ship's cabin, painting it with warm morning colors. Softness enfolded him. He became aware that he was not alone in the bunk.

"Hello again," someone said, warmly. And very nearby.

He managed a wan smile, feeling his head.

"Don't touch." True raised a sleepy head. "I bandaged that myself."

"How'd I get here?"

"I came back to see you on board the boat. But when I got here, somebody was just leaving the cabin. I yelled—he jumped out the forward hatch."

"Yeah. I remember that I heard something in the forward compartment. When I went in, somebody jumped me." He touched his aching head again.

"How're you feeling?"

"Awful. Why'd you come back?"

Her eyes were very blue as she came closer. "I didn't like the way our evening ended. Do you understand?"

"Bruce. Yeah, he wasn't looking so good."

"No, luv. I've been around this waterfront since I was a baby."

"OK. What then?"

She squared her shoulders, her blue eyes flashing: "Get a clue."

"If it's something I said..."

She leaned forward to bury her blonde head on his chest. "When I saw you covered in blood, it scared me. I thought I had lost you. Permanently."

"But..."

"Just listen. I was always the little urchin in Marci's shadow. My big sister had everything."

"But..."

"When I saw you lying there..." She said nothing more, but her eyes grew moist.

Kevlin was silent for a moment. "I think I understand," he said, adding, "You were with me last night? All night?"

"Watching over you."

"I thought....never mind," he said. "Er, it must have gotten pretty cold sitting all alone in that chair."

"Oh, yes." Her eyes turned mischievous. "I hope you didn't mind my joining you."

She leaned down to kiss him on the head.

"That make it any better?"

A glow suffused her features. "Try this, then." She kissed him on the mouth. It was a long, passionate joining of souls and it took his breath away.

"Just hold me," she whispered. "I want to lie here, just be with you."

Then he felt her fine blonde hair on his chest, her breath on his body, and they were together as the morning grew bright in the cabin.

2 7

THE NEXT MORNING, Kevlin headed straight to Tremain's office. He limped past the boatyard's workers, holding his breath as he passed through the perpetual haze of petrochemicals.

Tremain sat upright behind his desk as Kevlin barged in, his eyes riveted to the bandage on Kevlin's head.

Kevlin winced. "Someone surprised me."

"What I hear, serves you right."

"What'd you hear?" Kevlin looked over at True, who grimaced from behind her desk. She shook her head. Apparently True had only told Tremain about part of the evening.

Tremain angrily crossed his arms. "I got a call from Bush. Said the police found the door broken open, you two snooping around—and two bodies."

"You're blaming me?"

"You were snooping around behind my back." He shot an angry glance at True. "And as for you..."

"My fault entirely," Kevlin said, fighting back his temper. "I'll be leaving soon."

"You bloody well should. The sooner you get out of here, the sooner this stops."

"But first, you gave your word."

Tremain's face grew red with anger.

Kevlin pulled wrinkled papers from his foul weather jacket pocket. "Here are the notes for my next story. The one you agreed to help with."

"The keel again. Damn the keel."

"A deal's a deal." Kevlin straightened out the pages. "Now let's see the bloody secret design."

*   *   *

Tremain stomped ahead of them down the steps to the boatyard's Skunk Works. With all the overheads on, it seemed a different world from the shadowy land of the other night. Ignoring
the keel mock-up, he led them to a small room tucked into the
back.

Kevlin eyed the eerily glowing banks of computers. "How
about booting up your CAD program?"

"Understand me," Tremain said, sitting down at a keyboard. "I
agreed to help. But I'm not giving everything away."

"Just show me a display of the Swagwoman keel. I don't need
exact engineering measurements."

Tremain grumpily booted up a program in the computer, and
with a few taps of the keyboard, brought a full-color reproduction
of the keel to the monitor. And there it was: the secret keel.

"Beautiful. Magnificent." Kevlin paused.

"Now give me a hard copy printout, please."

Tremain grunted, hit a few more keys. As he waited pensively
for the printout, trepidation chased the anger from his face. "She
was my creation. Mine. I put everything I knew into her."

True laid a hand on Tremain's shoulder. "No one can blame
you."

"Something slipped by me," Tremain said. "Somewhere there
was a fatal flaw. I have to find it."

Kevlin was alert. "Fatal flaw? In the design?"

"No. Somewhere in construction, Bush's best intentions not-
withstanding."

"What are you saying?"

"The carbon fibers had to have had some contamination. The
epoxy didn't set right. Without a perfect bond..."

Tremain paused, breathing deeply. "They separated—and
broke apart. Damn, damn!"

"It's over," True said. "Don't go there any more."

"Marci..."

Tremain stared hard at Kevlin.

"And now—you're out of here!"

28

THERE WAS an uncomfortable silence in the car as True drove him to the airport. She seemed tense, driving with her head forward and her hands clenched around the wheel, her fingers white.

"Something wrong?" he asked.

"No," she said, too hastily. "Maybe I'm a little tired."

"Me, too. But I've got to get back. And face Sam."

"And crawl a little?"

"I have to work things out."

True braked hard, stopping the car at a waterfront overview of the Sydney harbor. She let the motor run. In the distance, an ocean-going sailboat was putting out to sea.

"What about us?"

Kevlin stiffened. "I don't know, exactly." It was a lousy answer and he knew it.

"Yeah, well, see you around, Yank," she said, bitterly. "Is that it?"

"It's not like that, True. "

"My sister?"

"I'm all tied up in knots inside."

He wanted to say more, but couldn't think of what.

He had growing feelings for this beautiful Sydney woman. But somewhere along the trail of heartaches and mysteries, he had lost so much of himself that everything he said, everything he did, felt wrong.

He pressed his hand to his aching head, managing to jar the scab in the process. "Ow."

"Still hurts, doesn't it," True said, putting her arm gently around his shoulders.

"Kevlin, you'll sort it out. Give it time."

"For right now, I'm in deep doo-doo."

"I still believe in you."

"Marci is...gone. Everything is upside down for me. I don't know what I've got left. Might be...nothing."

They reached the airport without speaking. Then she turned to him:

"Kevlin, I will see you again, won't I?"

Kevlin took a deep breath. "One way or another, I'll cover the race. And the race comes to Sydney."

She patted his arm. "I'll be waiting."

"See you then."

"Ta, love."

29

THEY HAD TRIED a combination of speeds and angles, but the hulk stubbornly refused to obey them.. Every time their velocity grew too high, it balked, threatening to shear back into the depths. It seemed to have a mind of its own, determined to the last to defy their efforts.

The rays of the setting sun illuminated the Sydney Heads. They were nearing their sad journey's end.

"Something dead ahead, skipper!" The First Mate pointed toward the entryway. The tugboat captain lifted his binoculars.

Long lines of boats steamed out from the harbor: vessels of all kinds and descriptions, powerful trawlers, sleek motorsailors, and large ocean-going sailing yachts.

Solemnly, they formed two rows, lining the way for the homecoming ship.

Through the center steamed the seagoing tug and the ruined hulk that once had been a proud racer. As they passed down the long row of vessels, captains and crew doffed their caps and bowed their heads. Boat flags flew at half mast.

A squadron of fighter jets flew from the blood-red sunset, thundering low to the water in the missing man formation: the pilots' way of saying farewell to a fallen comrade.

The Captain turned to gaze at the overturned hulk: the scarred remains that once had represented dreams of glory on the oceans of the world. It shouldn't have ended this way.

Thousands gathered to raise their hands in a final salute to the ruined craft, and Marci Whitman, their lost Golden Girl.

Behind and between them, the dark hull of a ruined sailboat twisted its bow from side to side in their wake.

As if it were *alive*.

30

HER FORCE slipping from her like life's blood, she dropped away from land, down into the frozen regions of the Antarctic.

Alone.

Just a tiny core with a few ebullient breezes left to her, she crept shivering and impotent into the lands where nothing else lived.

Her tyranny over the seas was spent; her tempestuous wings clipped.

The Lady.

Far behind her, in the skies she had ruled, the Southern Cross shone down from a clear, ebony vault, lighting the way for becalmed sailors.

The terrible, wild storm was gone.

SECTION
TWO

THE
RACERS
ASSEMBLE

31

AN ELECTRONIC WARNING DIODE blinked red. She flicked a hidden switch and a monitor glowed from one of *Corinthian's* many hidden security cameras. Sam Traveler hardly raised her eyebrows.

It was her prodigal editor, finally returning.

A knock on the bulkhead door. And there he was, sun-tanned, healthy, standing in the doorway. The arrogant son-of-a-bitch.

"Glad you could drop by." she said, acidly. "Have a nice vacation?"

Kevlin blinked twice as his eyes adjusted to the brightly lit captain's quarters. She was lying on her back on her exercise machine. Despite the air conditioning, a little sweat dripped down her forehead.

Time to take it slow. "Can we talk about this?"

"Really?"

"For openers, why'd you fire me?"

Very cooly: "You must've got it wrong."

"What?"

She sat up, wiping the sweat from her face with a small towel. Her eyes glowed deeply, her voice low. "Yeah, don't overthink it."

He made some sort of noise in his throat.

"Mr. Bear will fill you in."

Mr. Bear? First this snowjob and now Mr. Bear?

She turned her back on him, returning to her workout with a vengeance:

"Goodbye. Don't let my door hit your ass on the way out."

3 2

Despite the radio room chatter, Bear's head lifted momentarily as Kevlin slipped through the bulkhead door. He must have eyes in the back of his head.

"The boss lady has a way with her, don't she?"

Kevlin was not amused. "She needs a pill. Maybe two."

Bear sat upright, turning to face Kevlin. "You think you got troubles? Me? I got to set up a new Web site on your race."

"Don't call it my race. Not anymore."

Bear saw the look in Kevlin's eyes. "You've got to learn not to get so excited. Take things in stride. They could be worse."

"Yeah? I don't see how. *Mr. Bear.*"

`Bear just smiled. "Old buddy, you could be around full time."

"Aargh!" said Kevlin. He hit his fist on the bulkhead, making a booming sound.

"Deeply felt," Bear said He nodded toward the glowing computer terminal. "But you should know there are tons of people interested in the race."

Bear moved his mouse around, flipping through various web sites. "Sixteen sites already and growing. Most with chat rooms. All boiling over with theories." He cocked his shaggy head. "Hoo, ha! The Interweave knows all."

Kevlin glanced over, interested. What's getting the most play?"

"The conspiracy theory," Bear said.

He had a conspiratorial smirk on his face, obviously intended for Kevlin's amusement.

"Too many coincidences," Bear said, sitting back in his oversize office chair, putting his paws on his large belly, "Personally, I think they are barking up the wrong tree."

"Since when are you an expert?"

"On the Internet, everyone's an expert. Didn't you know that?"

Bear leaned forward. "Here's something: Did you know that when the storm came up, Marci was ordered to reef down?"

"And she told them to stick it."

"Yeah, but 50 miles-per-hour gale-force winds? And she *still* didn't reef down?"

"Neither would I!"

Bear was not to be put off. "I figure she must've been out of control, came beam-to on a big breaker and rolled the boat 180 degrees. Ever think of that?"

"I was onboard the wreck. Remember? The keel break wasn't at its weakest point. It broke several feet down. How do you account for that?"

Bear waved that aside, deep in his theoretical debate. "Keels broke before—in other races."

"Years ago, when the technology was new."

"Naw it's still going on. How about that one sailor who ran into a storm on his qualifying run. His boat flipped over when the ballast bulb fell off. They found his boat, but never found him."

"Different scenario," Kevlin said, softening his tone. He was talking about a buddy. "He had run his keel aground before he headed into the North Atlantic and there was a problem with how the ballast bulb was designed—it was not heavily bolted."

"Yeah, but remember that America's Cup? One racer actually broke its hull in half. Carbon fiber again." Bear sat back smugly, as if to affirm his case rested.

Kevlin clenched his fists, fighting back his anger. Time to switch subjects. "Anything else?"

"A bunch of advertisers are about to pull out. The race is starting to scare them."

Kevlin managed a bitter laugh. "No wonder La DL was so lathered up."

"Don't be so hard on Sam. Besides, she's got a plan." Bear sat back, expectantly, on his haunches.

"La DL did not deem fit to explain."

Bear managed a conspiratorial look. "Know what it is? What Sam really wants?"

"No." A sudden chill came over him.

"ESPN," Bear said, dropping the hammer delightedly.

"You're kidding!" Kevlin began, straightening up. "National TV—the all sports network? I'm not up to that."

"I don't know if I should share this with you, old buddy," Bear added. "You're gonna find out anyway, soon enough."

"They don't call you the Communications Center for nothing. So communicate."

Bear glanced about, then leaned forward. "You're not just going to be interviewed for a story or two. You're gonna do color commentaries. Be a real color commentator."

"No way. I've never done that."

"They point their finger at you and you talk. Live on camera. Colorfully."

"How tough is that?" He added, smiling: "Sam has already accepted on your behalf."

"Hell no! She couldn't."

"She could. And did. It's something in your contract." Bear was enjoying himself.

Kevlin was perspiring heavily now and it wasn't just the heat in the room.

Welcome back home. Stewed, screwed and tattooed.

"Our very own TV star," Bear intoned, obviously with relish.

"Fuck you. Fuck your television monitor. Fuck everyone."

It was not original, but heartfelt.

33

R ACE ALONE AROUND THE WORLD captured the
excitement of a bygone era, of giant sailing ships that roamed
the world's trade winds—and that once called New York home.

The significance of the racer's gathering place was neither lost
nor coincidental.

The area beside the historic South Street Seaport Museum was
the center of New York's famous 19th century port, when the
giant sailing ships flourished. Here were berthed the beloved
square riggers, the four-master *Peking*, and the full-rigged ship
Wavertree.

In the shadows of the historic vessels floated the world's finest
ocean racers in the world's best-promoted event.

Now a new fleet would set out from New York harbor to carry
their nations' flags around the world. It was the big-time of
world-class ocean racing, more widely publicized than the
America's Cup.

The public seemed fascinated by the steady stream of stories
revolving around a breathless, but emerging underlying theme:
Were these monster wind ships, in their quest to break records,
jinxed—and about to murder more mariners?

RAAW was different than anything that had gone before. With
dare-devil ocean racers at the helm, it would be sailed on the
most boat a single sailor could race—the 60-foot-long century-
class vessel.

There were no limitations of sail area, or other artificial cur-
tailments—the most daring oceanaut would win the race, provided that the boat held up "around the course."

That would include navigating the two traditional horrors of passage, the misnamed Cape of Good Hope and the infamous Cape Horn.

No one could overlook the dangers that lurked ahead. September's traditional North Atlantic storms were moving in early. The racers would have to rely on their speed, and a measure of luck, to get out of New York.

Presuming they could survive what the North Atlantic threw at them, they'd have to head off on the classic clipper ship route—across the equator to the bottom of the world.

*   *   *

The leaders probably would arrive in the first port, Cape Town, South Africa, toward the end of October—a run of nearly 6,800 nautical miles.

Cape Town would be the first of four stages, each progressively worse.

Leg Two swung them out past the Cape of Good Hope and down into the Roaring Forties, with its wild winds and menacing icebergs.

The Southern Ocean voyage would be wet, windy, and almost unbearably cold. To search for the violent winds that would power their boats to victory, some boats would brave going down into the Fearful 50s and even Screaming 60s.

Capsizing in the icy waters would be a constant danger as the racers pushed their boats for all-out speed. Some racers would not eat or sleep for days.

All would have to sail alone through the vast reaches of the Southern Ocean.

Adding to their dangers would be storms, rogue waves, fog, and huge icebergs.

Nearing the easternmost shelf of Antarctica, they would begin their ascent toward the Tasman Sea and Australia. By the time they neared the dreaded Bass Strait north of Tasmania, the sailors would be running on adrenaline.

But the treacherous waters beneath Australia with their extremely steep seas and fast moving wave patterns, would give them no rest. To win, the racers would have to ride wild waves with reckless abandon, risking capsize and broaching—that would result in the loss of their boats as well as possibly their lives.

The battered boats and sailors would find the end of the second leg in Sydney's beautiful harbor, after covering nearly 7,000 nautical miles from November 15 to about December 20th. The majority of the racers would arrive before Christmas Day.

Some might not make it at all.

There'd be a layover before the longest leg would run 7,200 nautical miles from Sydney, Australia, to Punta del Este, Uruguay, past the treacherous Cape Horn. Leg Three would begin February 1 and would take until early March.

Leg Four was the shortest for those still in the race: from Punta del Este back to New York, about 6,000 nautical miles. Here the racers would set sail out of Punta, follow the South American coastline across the equator, then up into New York.

The final racing leg was scheduled to begin April 1 and was expected to take less than 30 days, weather permitting. The winner would cross the finish line in New York harbor about April 30—after sailing around the world alone—for 27,000 miles.

There were 13 entries, the leading contenders culled from a fleet of 25 who had tried but failed to make RAAW finals months earlier. First prize was $5 million.

It was the world's toughest race: solo sailors, giant sailboats, racing unassisted and nonstop on the worst waters on earth— braving storms, giant waves and icebergs—as they raced each other around the world on only wind power.

Clearly, what lay ahead was a death race. Not all who set out would return.

Everyone was talking.

And it would begin in just four days.

35

THE COMPOUND was encircled with heavy wire fencing that in turn was wrapped in heavy canvas. The entrance was guarded by a steel door that echoed hollowly as Kevlin knocked. A guard in a red uniform and white gloves, carrying an automatic pistol, looked out suspiciously from a small peep window.

There was little question that the Pacific Rim wanted to keep what they had behind the shrouds a secret. Yesterday, in a practice run, their racer had encountered an unfortunate problem: its mast had broken.

They'd be on their guard about that.

"We have an appointment with Mr. Maginawa." Kevlin flashed his press card: "I'm Kevlin Star, with ESPN. This is my cameraman, Jock Radlevich."

The guard grunted, then lifted a tiny hand-held radio. He listened for a moment, then bowed to the authority of the voice at the other end. Turning, he led them through the gate into a canvas-covered tunnel and then into a windowless concrete building.

"Welcome to the media," said Sakko Shuro Maginawa, in a faintly bemused English accent. He bowed crisply and offered a white-gloved hand in greeting.

Maginawa was about 36 years old and nearly six feet tall, his jet black hair neatly lacquered in place. Countless hours of ballroom dancing and Kendo gave him a hard physical grace, tempered by his Oxford manner.

Today he wore a well-tailored red racing uniform, with the badge of the *Satari* sewn over to the left breast. He wore both the uniform and his role as host to the media with obvious relish.

"Thanks for having us," Kevlin said. He looked around with a sailor's practiced eye. "May I request, sir, that we get out of here to do the interview? On board the boat would be much better visually."

Sakko hesitated only for a moment. "Of course."

Score one for our team, Kevlin thought. Now they could get the first real look at the new boat the consortium had kept under wraps for so long.

And a look at some of its much-vaunted secret gear. Including the broken mast.

Why had it been so easy?

* * *

A white nylon superstructure enclosed the boat. It let in light, but obstructed any view from above.

"The brightness is OK," Jock confirmed, hefting his camera. Kevlin's strategy for getting the details of the boat was to move about from area to area as he interviewed Sakko.

The specific details would come in the medium or long shots.

"How about the port side?" he asked. That would be near where the mast failure had originated.

Sakko strode with a fencer's brisk pace to the boat's side, glancing at the missing chain plate.

A brief nod from the cameraman and Kevlin began:

"Today we are on board the new contender, the *Satari,* and with her skipper Sakko Maginawa. Yesterday, in view of our cameras, the racer spectacularly lost her mast. Sakko, what happened?"

"A sequence of events, starting with the chain plate, " Sakko said, disarmingly shrugging his shoulders. "Perhaps too much stress."

A little too glib, Kevlin thought as he saw Jock zooming in with the telephoto. He continued with his running commentary: "Here we have one of the innovative designs of the new racer: a built-in chain plate."

He saw Jock move forward for a close up. "On most racers, the chain plate is a massive stainless steel fitting. But what's this?"

"Carbon fiber, of course!" Sakko moved closer, then crouched beside the broken stub. "We can achieve the same strength as stainless steel, with far less weight, and integrate the design with the hull reinforcements by using carbon composite. But as you see, the top segment wasn't able to withstand the racing loads we began putting on it. We need a stronger plate."

"When did you know the mast was in trouble?"

"There was a noise, like a gunshot. I looked and saw the rigging curling up from the broken chain plate—all of a sudden, my mast looked like a buggy whip. Some fun, huh?"

"What did you do next?"

"I headed into the wind, trying to take the pressure off..."

"I was above you in our helicopter. I saw the top part of the mast break at the uppermost spreader. There seemed to be a puff of smoke....

"You saw that? Amazing!"

Kevlin continued: "...and your stick started to topple to starboard, followed by another puff of smoke and a break in the mast near the gooseneck. Question: what caused the smoke?"

"We don't know. Perhaps....the carbon exploded under pressure," Sakko said. "At the time of the break, we estimate a load on the chain plates of about three and a half tons. What you saw might have been carbon fragments bursting outward."

A sudden gleam came to his eyes. "What do you think? Is someone is trying to sabotage us?"

Kevlin was startled. "Let's go over to the mast step."

The two sailors walked to the mast: there were only a few feet sticking up from the deck.

Kevlin deliberately held his hand to the shards and pressed downward. "These are sharp!"

"Yes, like knives. One must be careful around carbon fiber breaks, Mr. Star."

There it was: The break had the same characteristics he had seen on *Jolly Swagwoman's* keel. There were sharp breaks on the inside and the smooth oatmealish gap surrounding them.

Kevlin took a deep breath: "Why is the outside of the break so smooth?"

"No idea, old man." Sakko's raised one eyebrow. "I'll have to check with our technicians."

Someone in red overalls and white gloves ran up to whisper in Sakko's ear.

"I think I have your answer. Our crew was grinding the outer rings to get the fittings out. Perhaps that accounts for what we see."

Kevlin didn't have time to pursue it further. "Will this cause the *Satari* to drop out of the race?"

The racer smiled engagingly. "We are prepared for all eventualities."

He grinned boyishly and led them to the edge of the deck. In the water below, in a Zodiac inflatable, were uniformed mechanics. On floats behind trailed the remains of the broken mast.

"When the mast went over," Sakko said, "it floated long enough for our team to tie it to some buoys. We'll send it to our research lab to analyze. Next time, we'll build it thicker and stronger. In a way, this is the best thing that could have happened. Much better now, than during the race."

Kevlin studied the broken spar. It was well over a hundred feet in length, certainly the biggest for a racing machine since the America's Cup.

While Jock got the mast focussed on videotape, Kevlin did a voice over:

"And there, in the water, is what remains of the *Satari's* carbon fiber mast. Obviously, the break at the chain plate would have weakened the mast system. But usually in such a case, the mast would just go overboard, without breaking. Sakko, what do you feel caused the mast to break twice the way it did?"

"Maybe in my enthusiasm I was carrying too much sail for the wind conditions," Sakko said thoughtfully.

"I looked up, and I just had the feeling: 'It's going to go.' Before I could ease the sails, or head up to reduce the pressure, it went.

"Just one thing..." Sakko paused for dramatic effect, with both hands outspread.

"And that is..."

"We were going like a flaming rocket." He clapped his hands together.

"You're saying *Satari* is a very fast boat?"

Sakko smiled broadly, then nodded.

Kevlin knew the racer would not give out details, but since Sakko had broached the subject, he might try one question: "To what do you attribute the *Satari's* speed?

"Oh, but you of all persons must know some of the reasons," Sakko said. He motioned for an attendant, who ran over carrying a magazine.

It was the new issue of *Megasail.*

"Your publisher was kind enough to Air Express us a prepublication copy," Sakko said smoothly, opening the magazine.

Kevlin inhaled sharply. Jock circled around with his camera.

Inside were explicit color photos, detailed and close ups, of the *Satari.* There was even an illustrated technical drawing showing her supposedly secret keel!

Kevlin tried to hide his surprise.

His magazine had the major scoop on the new superboat. But, obviously, he didn't. Why hadn't Sam told him about it?

He swallowed hard. He had a suspicion as to why he had been invited on board and allowed to tape: it was timed to happen just as the new *Megasail* article went on sale.

It was terrific promotion for the magazine. Damn Sam.

"But of course, you knew all about this, didn't you, old man?" Sakko was almost purring. He flipped through the pages.

"And here in the back is your article on the design of the Australian racer's keel. *Jolly Swagwoman.* Fascinating. Our technical people will want to study this."

"Thank you, Mr. Maginawa," Kevlin managed to choke out.

Furious, he faced the camera with as much poise as he could muster.

"This is Kevlin Star, for ESPN, on board the new Pacific Rim racer, the *Satari*, just 24 hours before the start of the biggest race of all time."

3 6

B EHIND HIM rose Manhattan's wall of glass and concrete but down here, at the water's edge, the world was primeval.

Kevlin's mood was lifting as walked the cobblestones to the old clipper ships, their tall masts spearing up toward the misty skies, tips obscured in fog. Though the old ships remained, the men who had sailed them were long gone, many to a watery grave.

From somewhere in the mists ahead came the rasp and whir of tools. Modern day man getting ready to do battle once again with the ancient, dark sea.

He passed along the shore, leaving behind the ghosts of the past for the specifics of the future. Two steps more and the fog parted on either side of him, rolling back like a curtain on a stage.

Before him set row upon row of racers. Electric lights strung about the boats like halos. Shivering in the cold, the crew members worked late in their compounds, making last-minute checks during this last night ashore.

Electronics and sensors were being tested and recalibrated; tension tests were run on the rigging, and, every inch of every hull was critically examined.

This was their last chance.

The last night in port.

When they left the protection of the harbor, the boats would enter the stormy North Atlantic Ocean and race nonstop to nearly the bottom of the earth—to Cape Town, South Africa.

After tonight, the boats were on their own.

And so would be the men and women who helmed them.

Despite their bravado, Kevlin knew that few had any illusions that the race would be anything but brutal, cold and exhausting.

Out there, anything could happen to them.

Injury. Illness.

Even death—alone and beyond help.

Another gust churned up the harbor and he shivered, less from the winds without, than from the morose ticking of his own mind.

*   *   *

The interview with Sakko had been inconclusive. Too much pressure on the mast. A problem with the layup.

Something like that.

The RAAW Director reported that the official race investigators had found no evidence of sabotage when they had been on board the *Satari*. Yes, he agreed that the breaks in the carbon fiber mast were unusual, but that was all they were.

There was a pattern here, if only he could find it.

And then there was the betrayal. His magazine had already had the information about the *Satari* and her secret keel. Big surprise. Why hadn't La DL dropped even a hint that it was coming? Why leave him hanging? And why had *Megasail* run his article and drawing of the *Swagwoman* keel in the magazine's back pages, obviously downplaying the whole effort.

Maginawa had practically snickered in his face. On camera.

Sam wasn't answering his calls. Including the one he had just tried 10 minutes ago. He had let the phone ring and ring on her personal number. He left a message. Fat chance she'd return his call.

A gust of raw wind whipped over the old waterfront; below him lapped dark waters.

Kevlin's shoulder was starting to ache, an old injury that flared up when he was tired.

Somewhere in the distance, the Staten Island Ferry chugged lonesomely; a fog horn sounded. The mists were wet on his face and hair as he stood looking silently over the waters.

Tomorrow the greatest race in history would begin.

Somewhere out there, and closer to home, powerful forces were gathering.

He wondered what would happen next.

37

B LUSTERY WINDS scoured the bleak waters into white-caps, but by 9 a.m. over one hundred thousand spectators shivered expectantly on the shores of the harbor.

Tens of thousands more watched in comfort from the shelter of skyscraper windows. In the harbor, small vessels manoeuvered for a better view. Fireboats gaily sprayed plumes of colored water in the air.

New York had turned out in grand fashion to see the racers off.

High over the harbor in the ESPN helicopter, Kevlin, Trish and Jock were already into their live telecast. Below, the racers jock-eyed near the starting line.

"There's the American entry—the one in red, white and blue," Trish announced excitedly. "*Solo Eagle.* Heading for the starting line."

As Jock's cameras picked out the individual racers, Kevlin added "and there's the New Zealand boat...The Australian boat... the *La Belle Paris* from France....and what's this?"

Below, resplendent in its blood red sails and hull was the *Satari.*

"Amazing! They got a new mast up....virtually overnight," Kevlin said with awe. "The Pacific Rim entry is back in the race!"

He lifted his binoculars. At the helm was Sakko Shuro Maginawa, in his smart red uniform, waving his white gloved hands at the crowds.

A roar of enthusiasm resounded across the harbor.

"Hold for a moment." The voice of Gordon, the program direc-tor, boomed in the crew's headsets. "We're cutting away for a crowd reaction." The TV monitor in the chopper showed a nun in her habit standing beside Pier 17, waving an American flag.

"Cut to wide angle." Gordon called for an overall shot of the fleet below. The Coast Guard had been at work, clearing a wide path for the racers. Behind the lines, the spectator fleet was forming at both sides of the route.

Each boat, large or small, was crammed to the rails with as many friends and relatives as each skipper could get on board. Rumors abounded that many movie, stage and literary celebrities were clustered on the bigger yachts.

From across the water came the amplified sounds of sea chanties sung from a choir on board the stern of the clipper, *Wavertree.*

"We're just minutes away from the start of this historic race," Trish said. "Kevlin, how are the conditions for the race today?"

"Great! Right now the wind is out of the north-northwest at about 25 knots, gusting to upward of 34 knots."

"Breezy."

"They were built for ocean racing conditions and, believe me, if a 25 knot wind is all they ever encounter, they'll be lucky. The wind direction is a good one, too: they'll basically be on a reach out of the harbor to the Atlantic."

He added, ominously: "The meteorologists say a low is expected to slide in after they're on the open ocean, so the going could get rough."

He added with a dramatic flourish, "Real rough."

Ho. Ho. He was starting to enjoy being a television color commentator. For a magazine writer, it was easy. And fun.

Jock's camera pulled back to pan the fleet spread out below, the Statue of Liberty, and the starting line stretched between two large motorsailors.

"On this first leg from New York to Cape Town," Kevlin said, his voice rising with excitement, "they'll race the storm to get to the Gulf Stream. The current there can give a boat more speed.

"At around 30 degrees north latitude," he continued, "they'll have to be careful of the horse latitudes. That's an area of the North Atlantic subtropical high where there's little wind. They'll want to skirt that."

Trish added, "And after that?"

"This time of the year, as the fleet enters the northeast trade winds, they'll have to watch for hurricanes approaching from Africa. The final approach to Cape Town can be tricky. And there's always the possibility this time of the year of a "black southeaster...."

There was a great blast of noise. Kevlin twitched involuntarily, then peered downward. It came from the liner, *Queen Elizabeth II*, anchored off Brooklyn, her horns adding to the excitement.

Below, the racers were lined up. Jock's camera was focussed on the lead RAAW ship. The Director had a flag in his hand, waving it.

A cannon boomed.

"*That's it!* The start of the race," Kevlin yelled into the mike.

The cameras were picking up frantic activity on each of the racing ships. In the background, the fleet began blowing its horns and whistles.

People cheered, shouted encouragement, and waved flags.

Slowly, the giant sails began to be hoisted and set. The great racers began to transform themselves into majestic wind machines, accelerating hard.

*   *   *

The first racer cutting across the line was *La Belle Paris*, followed closely by *British Victory. Solo Eagle* was in the middle of the pack.

Satari seemed to be having trouble getting going.

"Look out!" Trish shouted. She pointed below.

In the middle of the fleet, the steel-hulled St. Petersburg racer had picked up speed. The *Nastrovia's* skipper had her back to the helm, grinding the winches to adjust her sails.

Another boat crossed the *Nastrovia's* path and the racer's skipper yelled, "starboard" and waved frantically.

Too late.

With a crash, the heavy steel boat slammed into the other racer's forward section. Its mast rocked back and forth; Kevlin could see a hole where the steel boat had rammed the racer.

Water was rushing in.

"An accident—during the first minutes of the race," Kevlin said. "Let's hope no one was hurt."

The helicopter came closer, and Kevlin could see the holed boat was the Canadian entry, *Great White Express*. The boat's bow was already low in the water. Waves sloshed over its foredeck.

"Here's the rescue boat," Trish said. Below, the boat's crew plucked the sailor out of the water. He managed a wave.

"Apparently, he's unhurt and OK," Trish said.

"But his boat is gone. He's out of the race."

The St. Petersburg sailor shrugged and turned her back on the accident, her flaming red hair blowing in the breeze. She was intent upon getting the boat back into the racing fleet.

The only damage Kevlin could see to the brutish *Nastrovia* was a dent in her steel bow.

Kevlin paused a moment, letting the cameras linger on the racing fleet.

"There they go." he said.

"Next stop, Cape Town, South Africa—6,800 miles away."

38

IN THE ESPN race headquarters' weather center, the satellite scan had been recording worsening conditions.

The satellite information system showed an infrared picture of the North Atlantic.

No question about it: an Atlantic low was veering directly in the racers' paths.

With the front rolling in, the warm Gulf Stream currents would change. The racers would no longer get that fast-current boost— and the storm would pile up the stream, creating huge waves.

The center began broadcasting the warning: heavy weather ahead.

In the Antarctic regions, the Lady was stirring.

39

THE BOAT with the racing British green hull flew on its east south-east course. Lord Garwood wanted to cover as many miles as he could before the storm hit, forcing him to reef down.

His SATNAV position indicator showed he was behind the Frenchman's racer, but that didn't bother him.

There was still a lot of ocean left before they crossed the Equator.

He looked once to his sails to check them and to his cockpit control panel for the computerized results. No, she wasn't carrying too much sail. *British Victory,* though a heavily built boat, was plunging along nicely, not straining.

16.8 knots.

Not bad. He didn't want to push her too hard at this point in the race and risk stressing the gear unnecessarily. It was a long way around the world.

Obviously, his French friend didn't share his belief. Etienne was cracking on everything on he could, flying south with all speed possible.

True, the Frenchman was on a quicker route, but he'd be closer to the flow of the Gulf Stream than Lord Garwood cared to be. Special danger lurked there if a storm caught you.

The Gulf Stream flowed to the east toward England, like a hidden river, before it veered southward. Garwood looked for the invisible counter-current surrounding it that would boost his speed. He hoped to find it east of Bermuda.

If the storm veered and arrived too soon, it would rub stream and counter stream the wrong way, producing huge, unforgiving seas.

Waves that could be a disaster.

If a spot of low pressure was coming down over the Atlantic, well, hard cheese—just part of the sailing game.

Chin up. You took the bad with the good. In fact, the unpredictability of ocean racing was what gave it some of its special charm: excitement.

You definitely have to keep your head in the game. You had to think ahead and figure out what will move your boat best; you did it all. There was no engine to turn on, you only had the wind to power you. You used your concentration, your sailing awareness, balancing it all of with what you could do physically.

If you didn't do it, it wouldn't get done. In storms, high seas, high winds. It was you and your boat against the raw forces of the North Atlantic.

It was a wonderful challenge and a right proper test for a decent yachtsman. He'd spent years getting ready for this.

He settled back in his helm chair, steering by hand. From his radio, a legion of voices crackled, racers chatting away on the radio net.

A few were conspicuously absent; Etienne wouldn't answer any call, insisting upon silence to maintain his concentration and Sakko merely listened, not caring for the other racers' banter.

The Russian sailor was among the silent.

Odd. In New York harbor, she always had a few comments, sometimes scathing, in broken English.

She hadn't been heard from since the collision.

Garwood licked his lips thoughtfully. He'd keep up the pressure, mile after nautical mile, eating up the distance between them until the Frenchman's concentration flagged.

40

T HE *NASTROVIA* was proving to be a very wet boat indeed. Burdened with the massive weight of its own construction, the sloop didn't so much rise to meet the waves as to plow through them.

The Russian boat's low freeboard—which had appeared racy enough on the naval architect's blueprints—added to its problems.

Since the deck was low to the water, waves from all directions regularly boarded and swept its length, sluicing water into the cockpit, sometimes nearly filling it.

Nastrovia was on a southerly course, counter to the Gulf Stream, bashing straight through the confused waves. A lesser vessel might have been torn apart; *Nastrovia* paid no notice.

In the open cockpit, Anna Polin stolidly braced herself against the wheel, her heavy rubber fisherman's gear dripping, her long boots half filled with water. Her red hair was pasted against her head and the cold had begun to gnaw at her bones. She managed a grin: she had unshakable faith in her boat's strength and capability.

It was made of steel. And a special steel at that.

Her husband had been one of the soldiers sent to Afghanistan, a godforsaken battlefield from which he, and a lot of others, had never returned. She had turned some of the weapons of that war into an instrument for peace: the *Nastrovia.*

Anna was a dockworker in the St. Petersburg boatyard, one of many comrades who built and repaired fishing vessels. When the yard received a shipment of steel plates forged from melted-down battle tanks, she claimed them. and she and fellow workers had built the metal racer.

Nastrovia might be sluggish in the water, but she was monumentally strong. Like the battle tanks she was forged from.

And she had an extra card up her sleeve.

Anna had sailed in the frigid wastelands of the Baltic Sea. After those tormented waters, the North Atlantic was almost balmy.

Where the cold did touch her, she had will power, the sturdy blood of her forefathers—and vodka.

She hadn't had funds for an expensive SATNAV system and the constant salt bath had gotten below and put out what electrical equipment she did have, including her old Ham-band radio. Anna had discovered that when she last tried to get the hourly weather.

Nada.

She was alone and voiceless on the sea—and taking on water. Several of *Nastrovia's* seams forward were ruptured where she'd smashed into the other boat.

She'd already stuffed the hairline leaks by hammering in small wood pieces and calked that up with whatever else she could find to stop the water flow. She could slow it, but not turn it off.

At the next port of call, she'd have to check over the bow area, particularly around the forward anchor well and the stem fittings. Some new welding would take care of everything. That was how you fixed steel boats. Easy.

Right now what did a little water matter?

The bilge pumps could handle it. *Nastrovia* was tough enough. She was tough enough.

Anna and her boat had already survived a challenge that had broken a lesser ship and that was her secret. Anna had calculated the odds: If other ocean competitions were any indicator, the racers would drop out, one by one, victims of the sea, with cracked hulls, torn rudders, shattered keels and broken masts. They were, after all, plastic boats. Siberian frozen snot. Breakable.

She grinned lopsidedly, patting the rusty side of the cold steel cockpit. *Nastrovia* was metal and stronger than the rest. He would last the distance.

Anna was practically assured to be the winner.

She congratulated herself with another sip of vodka.

41

H E BENT HIS HEAD to listen to the sound of his boat's wake. It had a slight sizzle to it, no burbles. He had his water ballast trim right now, bow slightly down, stern up and no water dragging from the transom.

That meant speed, and speed was what the red boat was all about.

Sakko Maginawa was pleased. If anything, he was holding his vessel back. It was a part of the overall strategy his leaders had decided upon.

Satari had been designed for high-speed racing, and certainly the Pacific Rim conglomerate had the technology for that these days. They had learned.

Their scientists had watched the Americas Cup races, first hopeful, then horrified, as accidents befell the rival boats. A carbon fibre racer from Australia had actually cracked in two and sank. But the scientists did not walk away empty handed.

The Pacific Rim had turned their computers to work on the America's Cup data. His consortium tested mathematical models in simulated sailing conditions. Their performance had been pitted virtually against all other known blue-water racers.

They had arrived at a conclusion and converted it into a percentage: *Satari* would outperform the Societe Nautique boat by about 10 percent; the Royal Portsmouth Yacht Club sloop, by 12, and the independent American racer by about 18.

The rest didn't really matter.

He lowered his goggles and checked his position by the SATNAV: he was in the center of the fleet, well behind the leader, just where he wanted to be.

His course lay east south east, with the speeding French boat to his starboard. The English boat, showing a surprising turn of speed, was to his port, on a more easterly course. God knew where the Russian boat was, but he didn't care much—it was a rusty slug, anyway.

Always the careful technician, he once again brought up the satellite weather forecast from his consortium's private weather consultant. The computer glowed in vivid red and orange hues, showing the Atlantic low sliding toward his route. Not good. There was little chance of outrunning the gathering storm, but he could get as much out of the storm's eye as possible.

He'd stay toward the east and clearer water. Let the others battle the risky waves. He had the speed to avoid them. He brought up the latest infrared satellite photo. Yes, he could see the warmer flow of the stream, right where he wanted it.

With his white-gloved hand, he pressed a button and a hatch slid open. A lexan panel swung up with the hissing noise of small hydraulic pistons. This was the heart of the his sailing operation. Here he could hoist and trim all sails hydraulically. The lines were led below decks by sheaves; no regular winches were on board, electronic or otherwise.

He could barely suppress a grin. The "secret" gear above deck that the ESPN cameraman had so carefully videotaped had been a dummy set. The real gear was internal.

His hands lingered over the console: Here was where his group's technology shone. With a punch of a button, Sakko could summon forth computer programs to set the sails for him, instantaneously matching wind and wave conditions, calling forth the best sail trim and line tension. *Satari* could fly.

His ultra-secret carbon fiber sails were drawing well. Their strength was greater than any other sail ever devised.

His new mast was carbon fiber as well, but of a different design. It had been waiting for him all along. They had replaced the broken one overnight.

This was the correct mast—the one meant for the race.

Unlike the mast that had been splintered so showily in front of the television cameras in the harbor, this one was designed not to break. This one was designed to *win*.

42

H E SETTLED TO THE WHEEL, feeling the great machine thrust forward. *Solo Eagle* was handling well.

Corky Bowman's plan was to plunge eastward of the main thrust of the Gulf Stream, then down to the Equator, eventually to get onto the northeast trades.

Solo Eagle was one of the underdogs in the race, along with the *Nastrovia*.

While other racing clubs were backed by corporate conglomerates and all the money they could spend, his entry was virtually home-built with only a few modest grants. She had no exotic alloys. No high tech materials, no computers.

What she did have was wood. High tech wood—light veneers held in place and encapsulated by epoxy resin. Very strong, very light. Light meant speed.

And deep below, she sported a special keel.

Corky could hardly stop grinning: His boat might prove to be just as good as the corporate ones.

A chiming noise from his old wind-up alarm clock interrupted him. He put his boat on automatic pilot and dashed below to turn on the Ham radio.

The dots and dashes came: November Mike November, the call sign for the high seas offshore weather forecast out of Portsmouth, Virginia.

He bent his head to listen carefully.

It was as he had feared.

Bad storm rising.

Damn. A glance at his charts told him he'd bear the worst of it.

43

IT WAS PAST FIVE in the afternoon. Outside the office port-hole, rows of sailboat masts swayed in rhythm to a Pacific breeze.

Kevlin's eyes adjusted to the dim light of the *Megaboat's* communications center as he slipped through the bulkhead door.

Despite the radio room chatter, Bear's head lifted momentarily. He was hunched over the glowing display of his computer screen, tapping keys with two fingers.

"Great to be back, huh?" Bear said.

He must have eyes in the back of his head.

"Yeah," Kevlin answered bitterly. "Back here. Instead of being over there. You know, to cover the race. In person, like real journalists do."

"Too bad about South Africa."

"For Chrissakes," Kevlin was angry. "The dragon lady hired a South African free lance writer to cover the actual arrival. My story."

"It figures." Bear rumbled sympathetically. "Sam don't have to fly you over, so it's cheaper that way."

"So La DL is tightening things up. And my assignment on Leg 1 got the ax."

Bear managed a grin. "Well, instead of running off on assignments you could actually do some work around here. Like me."

Bear saw the pained look in Kevlin's eyes.

"You've got to learn not to get so excited," he said. "Take things in stride."

"Like you?"

"Sure. I get to play with new electronics gear. Very soothing. And I got a new job. Set up a web site on your race."

"It's not my race. Not any more."

"Have you checked the Internet lately?"

"No. Been too busy."

"More news, then." Bear pointed a hairy finger toward the computer:

Feared Missing at Sea

NEW YORK (AIP)---Concern grew today for Etienne Le Brun, the well-known French ocean racer, now overdue on his 7,000-mile race down the North Atlantic.

Le Brun lost communications with Societe Nautique three days ago during the Race Alone Around the World's first leg from New York to Cape Town, South Africa.

His new boat, *La Belle Paris*, was considered a leading contender in the 33,000 mile race.

A RAAW spokesperson said that the racing fleet had encountered a North Atlantic gale the second day out of harbor.

Racers and vessels making the passage to Cape Horn have been alerted to look for his marine blue racer.

"Just came in," Bear said. "No SOS calls, either. We'd have heard on our radio network.

"EPIRB signals?"

Bear shook his head. Nothing.

He scratched his beard and began to put the story on the Megasail web site. He looked up for just a moment:

"Kev, what are his chances?"

Kevlin stared at the news story, lost in memory. He knew first hand what it was like.

The upturned hull of Jolly Swagwoman, low in the hungry sea. He was aboard, hanging on desperately. Cold, wet. Waves roared over him. Hypothermia setting in. Shivering. Desperate. Alone.

"Kev?"

"Not good." Kevlin said reluctantly. *"Not good at all."*

44

A WALL OF WATER rushed at him, slamming into the boat's port quarter.

"Oh, shit!" was all Corky Bowman had time to utter before his boat pitched wildly. Water clawed at the beam, cascading into the cockpit. *Solo Eagle* twisted agonizingly, foamy water covering the deck and cockpit.

Corky held his breath as she popped free and began to plunge down the back side of a wave. Smoke arose from the automatic pilot.

He shook his head: He had only one option. If the autopilot couldn't steer his boat, he'd have to. No matter how long it took. He unhooked the overheated, locked up automatic pilot and he took over the helm to fight the storm.

And there he stayed, alone, hour after hour, day after day. So long as he stayed at the helm, his boat was safe; so long as he kept her bow aligned with the waves, she would stay afloat.

All he had to do was stay awake.

*   *   *

By the twelfth hour, he could not longer remember what to do. Left ... right...what was the heading through these monsters?

He found himself falling in and out of consciousness, awakening only to steer desperately away from an overtaking growler.

He made the only decision he could: he could steer no longer; the boat would have to fend for herself.

Going forward in his safety harness, he balanced his boat as best he could, adjusting the tiny amount of sail he could keep up.

After lashing down the steering wheel, he went below to collapse.

He knew what lay ahead: what racers called a "suicide sleep."

He slept like a dead man, but only for 20 minutes at a time. When his jarring alarm clock timer rang, he roused himself, somehow, up again—to steer frantically.

Toward the third day, that no longer worked.

When he awakened, the storm had blown itself out. He was amazed: somehow, he and his boat had survived. It was not without damage: the water had risen dangerously in the bilge, necessitating a hasty pumping by hand.

But basically, his boat was intact—and still racing.

He had lost time so there was no choice but to remain at the wheel. He turned his single sideband radio up loud—to help him stay awake.

Sixteen hours after the storm, more than five days after his gear had failed him, Corky Bowman headed toward the finish line, with only the stars to follow, and a dream to steer by.

*   *   *

Garwood plunged through the storm in good shape and it was on the 26th day of the race that he saw his first boats.

They weren't racers.

Six minutes to the second after his first sighting, a helicopter came out of the clouds, its speaker booming over the water. "Welcome to South Africa."

Lord Garwood fumbled for the radio. "Where do I lie?"

The answer when it came nearly broke him; his hands shook so hard he dropped the receiver.

"First! You are the first to finish!"

By the time he sailed into harbor, he had recovered enough to stand tall beside his steering wheel, a commanding figure waving his watch cap at the television cameras.

A spectator fleet closed about him, yelling their congratulations, honking their boat horns. Speeding inflatables, their gunwales filled with gawkers, dodged in and out of his path.

A cannon boomed as he crossed the finish line.

*   *   *

When his red racer finally pounded toward the finish line, he was in second place.

A distant second, actually.

Storm or no storm, Sakko grimly was forced to conclude that *Satari* was not as fast as the computers had calculated. His consortium would not permit another disgrace.

They were, in truth, a grim lot when it came to loosing.

Perhaps the onboard computers would have to be recalibrated.

He desperately hoped it was as simple as that. And that the problem was not more fundamental—a flaw in the design.

*   *   *

It was nightfall when Corky Bowman pushed the baseball cap back from his weary head.

"Where do I lie?" he yelled to the lone boat that came out to greet him.

"Third. You're third," the skipper called across the waters. "*British Victory* and the *Satari* came in hours ago."

Bowman felt a flush of surging joy. His home-built racer had not only survived heavy weather in the North Atlantic— but was faster than he ever hoped it would be.

He leaped into the air, yelling joyously.

45

PHILIP HARKKEN, of the *New York Post,* irritably waved his hand. It was unseasonably warm on the aft deck of the old square rigger, *Wavertree,* in New York's South Street Seaport Museum. His brow was covered in perspiration, but he was not the only one feeling the heat.

RAAW was facing the world's press.

"Answer my question," he demanded. "Will the race continue?" He leaned forward, tape recorder in hand.

"Absolutely!" The Director stood ramrod straight. "Stage Two, around the Cape to Sydney, will commence as scheduled."

"What about the missing boats?" It was Bryon McBoylum, the noted boating editor for the *Times*.

"We've just received confirmation that the Russian boat is still maneuvering under sail, and lies about 300 miles out of port."

There was a gasp among the crowd. "*Nastrovia* is in basic seaworthy condition, but her radio and electronics are out."

"A passing freighter made contact," the Director continued. "The skipper reports the vessel is taking on water at about 60 liters per hour from a seam opening up in the storm, stemming apparently from the collision in New York harbor. She has made temporary repairs and the pumps are handling it. Anna Polin expects to make port in about 36 hours."

Cameramen edged closer to the Director; spectators on the dock at the impromptu press conference offered a spattering of applause.

"Any news about Etienne Le Brun?" It was the *Post* reporter again.

"We're receiving no readings from *La Belle Paris's* on-board transponder. Neither has Argos. We have, of course, sent up search planes; the French government has their own planes criss-crossing the area."

He looked around carefully. "No results."

"Do you think his vessel sank?" a reporter asked.

"We're reporting him missing only. There is still hope."

"Would you know if he got to his life raft?"

"His life raft carried an EPIRB. Had he been able to activate it, we could home in right away."

"Sir. Have you received any signals?"

"Regrettably, none."

The tabloid reporter cleared his throat. ""After all these problems—the loss of the Australian racer during trials and now the Frenchman—hasn't this become a death race?"

"No!" The Director's face flushed with anger, but he held his body with military erectness. "I have talked personally with the lead racers already in port at Cape Town. I can assure you that they are raring to go."

"So the race will continue?"

"All the way!" he thundered. He gave a thumbs up signal.

There was applause from the spectators. The Director stepped back from the interview area. On cue, the band struck up a marching tune.

The news conference was over.

The next day, the tabloids had their day. "French RAAW racer feared lost! Death Race to continue."

46

THE CAMERA panned slowly. Fascinated and obsessed, he watched, again and again.

Tens of thousands of spectators jammed the Sydney pier to admire the Australian wonder boat and to meet the Golden Girl of sailing.

Flags fluttered, a brass band played.

The camera panned to her as she stood on tiptoes with her small hands on the oversized wheel and gave him a dazzling white grin—the sort the press doted upon.

Marci Whitman.

It hurt to look at her, she was so beautiful, so alive, so full of hope.

The crowd cheered as *Jolly Swagwoman* swung away from the dock and out into the Sydney Harbor. Across the waters, the giant sails of Sydney's Opera House glinted red in the morning sun.

That left only one thing more—what her fans had been waiting for.

The camera zoomed in as she called across the water,

"Ta, love!" She blew them a kiss.

"Ta, Marci," thousands lovingly thundered back, clapping and cheering.

Then she sailed away.

Forever.

*   *   *

Kevlin reached forward and touched the recorder's replay button—and once again the screen lit up. His eyes blurred and filled with tears.

The camera panned slowly.

Tens of thousands of spectators jammed the Sydney pier...

47

THE ROARING 40S earn their name from the peculiar noise the relentless winds make as they blow ceaselessly over restless seas.

Far from any land, unrestricted by any land mass, the seas built up massively to actually roar in their world of ice and cold. Titanic forces of storm and sea vie for dominance.

Huge waves some as big as four or five story buildings scour the seas.

In the Roaring 40s, no sailor could look forward to anything but a brutal and punishing ride. All would have to sail as hard as they could by leaving as much sail area up as the boat could stand. That meant surfing day and night and risking a capsize, broach or pitchpole, in bone-numbing cold and iceberg-filled waters.

A solo sailor venturing into its icy maw could die many ways: by drowning, by freezing, by being washed overboard, by being crushed under a capsizing boat or iceberg—or, the worst of all—the horrible white death of slowly freezing until dead.

It was in the Roaring 40s that lay the second leg of the Race Alone Around the World.

*   *   *

In the lead, Lord Garwood swung boldly out of Cape Town on a south south easterly course, making passage past the Cape of Good Hope, and down into the Roaring 40s.

Ahead of him lay the chill waters of Antarctica, where the vague shape of icebergs shambled through the night.

* * *

The *Satari* was in second place. And there was nothing he could do about it. All of the computers and the models and the mathematical probabilities couldn't close that gap.

Sakko glanced up once again to check the straining carbon fiber sails. Yes, the new computer was getting all that it could out of optimal sail settings.

There wasn't enough speed left in the hull to make a difference. That left just one thing. One desperate, suicidal possibility.

So when his radio flashed, he wasn't surprised. He'd been expecting the orders, preparing for the worst.

His new heading would take him deeper—down past Roaring 40s and into the Furious Fifties and Screaming Sixties.

Toward the end of the earth.

* * *

The New Zealand entry, Sidney Wellington, in his *Black Magic Flyer*, had moved up a place with the loss of the Frenchman.

His boat was the latest shape for speed: flat deck with an extremely wide beam. His fellow racers called it the "aircraft carrier." But the wide beam was no joke: it made his huge cargo of water ballast more effective by providing more leverage.

There was no question that once he got his machine set up, it was astonishingly fast. The problem was, it could be unstable. He had found that out on the storm on the North Atlantic on Leg One.

If he were to round up into the wind, or come beam to on a wave, all that water ballast on one side would make his boat tip. It was a harrowing thought, for if *Black Magic Flyer* were ever to flop over, it would not come up again. The flat deck would hold it in the water.

If he were lucky, he'd be up on top beside it. Then again, maybe not.

But it was a boat that could win, and winning was what ocean racing was all about. Luck was still a factor in winning these races. The harder you pushed, the luckier you got.

Sid was pushing his luck hard on an easterly course, his black boat surfing, when there was a blur of white on the starboard bow and a grinding noise.

The boat canted violently.

*   *   *

It was unbelievably cold at the wheel. Corky Bowman preferred to self-steer *Solo Eagle* as much as possible in the big waves. Though he had managed to scrounge up two new automatic pilots in Cape Town, he was determined to save them for later in the race, when inevitably, the grinding pace took its toll.

He couldn't see much beyond the bow of his boat. Spray from the huge growlers, torn off by the screaming wind, hit his face like bullets.

He was checking the compass and his position when the burning sensation came to his fingers again.

He pried his right hand off the stainless steel wheel and inserted the fingers in his mouth. When they warmed a bit, he put them into his chest pocket.

While one hand thawed a bit, he steered with the other.

He had forgotten gloves. He just hadn't thought of them when he left. Now his hands were freezing and the weather would only get worse.

He snapped on the autopilot, then ducked below to find some extra wool stockings. When he returned to steering, he put his stockings over his hands. With duct tape, he lashed them around his wrists.

They were slippery, but the improvised mittens would keep the frostbite away. They were wool. Wool would remain warm even when it got wet.

He was congratulating himself on his ingenuity when he smelled a peculiar odor, above the pungent tang of the sea.

He sniffed again. No, it wasn't the socks.

It was fresh water.

A lot of it.

Oddly, inexplicably, here in the middle of an ocean of salt.

48

"MAYDAY, Mayday, Mayday!" The call boomed over the ship's radio.

"I hear you loud and clear. Go!" It was the Australian racer, lying in 5th place.

"This is Sid Wellington in *Black Magic Flyer.* I am taking on water. This is an emergency. Repeat, an emergency."

"How long can you stay afloat?"

"Can't tell." The voice came in a rush now. "I hit something. There's a big gash in the starboard bow."

"Can you plug up the hole?"

"...Too big. Water's pouring in..."

"Where are you? Repeat, Sid: What is your location."

There was a howl of static, a faint cracking, then nothing more.

*   *   *

"He should lie behind me, somewhere south." It was Corky Bowman in the *Solo Eagle.*

"Better get him fast!"

The Australian was in charge of the emergency net. "Neither *British Victory* or *Satari* are answering."

"You got his exact...?"

There was silence.

Then, "Damn. That was close."

"What happened?" crackled the radio.

"Barely missed them."

"What?"

"Something in the water, lying low."

"What?"

"There's that fresh water smell all around here."

"Ice...smells like fresh water."

"Yeah." There was a pause in Bowman's radio transmission.

"I can see something now. Bergy bits. In fact, I'm surrounded."

49

"IS THERE ANY INFORMATION on the missing racer?" The mood of the press conference was openly hostile.

"No further word," said RAAW Director Phillip W. Harken. "We have to classify Etienne LeBrun as missing at sea."

"Will there be further searches?"

"No. We've done all we can."

There were some raised eyebrows among the reporters. Zoom lenses buzzed noisily for close-ups.

"The New Zealander?"

"Two of the racers are answering his Mayday calls. They should reach him in a matter of hours."

"Is he OK?"

"We'll know shortly. He's been out of touch since he called in that his boat was taking on water. I imagine he's been a little busy."

"Doing what?"

"Probably...surviving."

A snicker of cynical laughter swept through the media group. Then it was back to business.

"Sir, what are you doing to rescue them?"

"We've got the U.S. Navy cruiser *Norfolk* rerouted for Sydney harbor."

"A nuke?" It was the New Zealand reporter. "Not bloody likely."

Harken cleared his throat. "I understand that there are difficulties in getting our U.S. Navy rescue ships into Australia or New Zealand ports. But this is a rescue mission."

"No nukes here," shouted someone. "Keep 'em out.!"

Another tack: "Other than a nuclear-powered warship, what do you have to rescue sailors?"

"Australian Search and Rescue."

"The race puts them into danger, too, does it not? "

Harken frowned. "Yes, but what's search and rescue for? That's their job."

"So the Death Race will continue unrestricted?"

"I abhor that term. The Race Alone Around the World will continue, yes."

"Next port of call: beautiful Sydney. See you there."

It was his parting shot. The Director turned on his heels and marched away from the microphones.

The next day the tabloid headlines read:

"Death Race Nearing Sydney."

SECTION
THREE

DISCOVERY

50

THEN THE AIRCRAFT was on the ground and Kevlin moved quickly through Sydney customs.

He felt a hand grab his arm. "Here, Kev. Hurry."

It was True.

"We should move right along," she said urgently, steering him directly out to the exit. "I'll tell you more later."

"Am I a fugitive or something?" Kevlin half joked as they emerged from the airport.

"No joke," she said, starting the car and jamming it into gear.

"The police? Do they have a warrant?"

"You were warned not to leave the country."

God almighty! Kevlin groaned.

"They have your fingerprints from the foundry."

"I gave them a statement."

"You were the first to discover the bodies. That automatically makes you a prime suspect."

True drove hard, constantly checking her rear view mirror. "They're acting very odd these days, Kev," she said.

Kevlin looked hard at her as she said, "They think they have a link."

"Oh, really? What?"

"You, I'm afraid."

She continued: "They've been under a lot of heat to solve the murders. A big stink. Marci had a lot of friends, including some of the young turks in the police. Anyone who falls into their hands will not have an easy time of it."

The seriousness of what she said hit home. He needed to stay away from their tentacles for as long as possible. They'd take him in for questioning, if he was lucky. If not—incarceration.

Or worse.

It was a break that he had booked a flight at the last minute and arrived in Sydney over a weekend. Any police check of incoming passengers would be snafued by the crowd.

That wouldn't last long.

"I've still got a job to do, but I can't go to a hotel," he said. "Or anywhere I have to show my passport. Or use a credit card that they can use to track me."

The car abruptly pulled into a back alley. True peered cautiously about, then motioned to Kevlin. They walked quickly to the boatyard.

"I should warn you," True added, "Grandfather has a surprise."

"Will I like it?"

"If I tell you, it won't be a surprise, will it?"

*   *   *

As True opened the back door of the shop, they were engulfed in petrochemical smells, and one more: the smell of burning gases.

Kevlin sniffed the air. Something familiar. Unexpected—and faintly sulfuric.

"Something's wrong," he said, striding over to workers with gas acetylene torches, cutting away a portion of a cruising boat's transom.

"What?" True asked.

"Damn. I can't tell— yet."

"Welcome... but what interests you here?" Tremain came down the steps, observing Kevlin's concentration. "We're just doing a little work on a cruising boat."

Interrupted. Kevlin shook his head. He didn't know.

If Tremain had any questions about the police inquiry, he was not mentioning it.

"So you've come to cover the race," Tremain said. "I thought you were odd-man out on your magazine."

"It was all about budgets," Kevlin tried to explain. "Sam finally relented after she saw what the free-lance writers were coming up with for her precious magazine and she finally loosened the purse strings and sent me. So...what's new?"

"One boat is sinking. The New Zealander."

"I heard before I left. Another accident?"

"No, he hit GOK.

"GOK?"

"God Only Knows. Probably, ice. Rescuers are on the way. Up to their gunwales in ice. And now two boats are out of communications somewhere in the Southern Ocean."

"Not good."

Tremain shook his head.

"We've been following their transponder signals. Lord Garwood's radio is out. RAAW can't contact him. We don't know about the other."

As Tremain talked, Kevlin continued to stare at workers with torches, cutting through the fiberglass. "Tremain, I have to ask you. I've been running this through my mind a lot."

"Ask away."

"There's a linking element: all the boat accidents had one thing in common. Carbon fiber composite construction."

"That we know."

"I keep coming back to that peculiar break on *Jolly Swagwoman's* upturned keel. Part melted, part jagged. I saw it —but whatever happened to her hull?"

Tremain looked guiltily at True, who explained: "Grandfather couldn't just let the hull stay out there. He sent a tugboat to bring the hulk back in and we tied it alongside the pier.'

"The authorities were interested," Tremain said, "and so were we. In doing some testing."

True added: "But the darndest thing. One night, someone must have come along with a power hacksaw. In the morning, we found the keel stub gone.

"Maybe a souvenir hunter got it." Tremain was caught by bitter memories.

"But why would anyone do that?" True asked. "It was just a black mass, about a foot and a half high."

"Just a stub," Tremain added. "Why would anyone would want to steal it?"

Kevlin kept watching the boatyard workers with the welder's torches. They had smoked welder's face shields on and wore welder's gloves. The torches had been adjusted to the hot blue flame, and, they moved the flame over the fiberglass. It sizzled and smelled.

And melted.

*   *   *

"Heat," said Kevlin. "That's it. You use heat!"

"Oh, that." Tremain said, nonchalantly. "There are two ways to cut fiberglass. One's with a reciprocating saw. The other's an old outback boatbuilder's way—a welder's cutting torch. Nothing fancy, but it works."

"But a welder's torch is to cut steel."

"It's quicker this way."

Kevlin moved forward, hardly believing what he saw. The fiberglass melted under the torch's heat and puddled in runs. As it cooled, it was lumpy.

"Looks exactly like the break I found. The outer layer."

Tremain stepped forward. "This is resin laid up in fiberglass. Marci's keel was epoxy laid up carbon fibers."

Kevlin's mind was racing. Sure, the epoxy-carbon layups were stronger than steel. But they had their Achilles's heel, so to speak.

Even the toughest epoxy would soften and melt under heat.

Like this. Both melted under the welder's torch.

True's eyes widened: "Do you think a diver went underwater and torched the rudder of *Kiwi Kubed* and the keel on *Jolly Swagwoman*?"

"No, no!" Tremain was adamant. "A torch would send up a stream of bubbles. There'd be smoke and noise. Anyone would've spotted it for sure."

"They didn't use a bomb."

"No. An explosion would have shattered the keel. Into a million pieces."

"But I saw the same sort of layering...lumpy, on the outside. As if melted by heat."

"Exactly. And I don't know how it was done. I just know it was done."

In frustration, Kevlin slammed his fist against the boat. "Ow," he suddenly yelled, angry at the pain. The cut had only partially healed and started to bleed again.

"But the inner area was sharp and jagged, like a knife. That's where I sliced my hand open."

"And yet the outer area...."

"Yeah. That I don't understand why the outer area was smooth, like it had been melted. And the inner area was sharp, splintered enough to cut me."

"Melted." The thought gripped Tremain. "Marci had a partially melted carbon fiber keel."

"And you were on the Kiwi boat," True added. "That could have killed you. It had broken rudders."

"The link between the two," Kevlin said, "was the peculiar break in the carbon fiber. One in the rudder, one in the keel."

"Exactly the same type of break," Tremain said. "Exactly. I hauled the Kiwi boat as soon as you got it back to the dock. Smooth on the rudders' outsides, jagged on the insides."

"Yes, and on the day he was killed," Kevlin continued, "Bruce told me he was onto something. We found him at the foundry that made both the keel and the rudder...along with the dead foundry worker.

"Both knew something— and were killed for it."

"That's it, then," Tremain thundered. "The truth at last. Not design, not construction. *Sabotage.*"

"But who?" asked True. "Who would do such a thing?"

"I don't know—and I don't think they're done yet," Tremain said.

Kevlin had a sudden dread. "Who's leading in the race?"

"Lord Harwood, in his British racer," Tremain said. "Even presuming you're thinking what I think you're thinking, there's no way to get a message to him," Tremain cautioned. "His communications are out."

"Even if we could prove anything." Kevlin thought a moment. "What's the weather?"

"A Force Five storm coming through," True said. "With fog banks."

"A perfect setup," Kevlin said, angrily. "The others died in the cover of storms."

"Even if you are sure, how can you warn Harwood?" True was worried. "There's no way to get a message to him."

"Provided you are still free to do so," Tremain added, "The police probably have run through the airline passenger lists by now and will want you for questioning—and maybe more. If you're around, they'll catch up with you for certain."

"Chartering an airplane would be out," True said. "You'd be caught the minute you flashed your identification."

*   *   *

"There might be a way," Kevlin said. He began pacing hard now, his thoughts tumbling out. "If I tracked him down as he came in."

"By sea?"

"Garwood's automatic beacon is still going, so you know his position here," Kevlin explained. "You could give me his heading and location by radio."

"True enough. But that would mean you'd have to go to sea and stay out there for a while. And wait."

"A power boat?" True shook her head even as she spoke the words. "No, we don't have anything in the boatyard with enough range."

"As he closed in," Kevlin added, "I could pick him up on long-range radar.

"Even in fog."

Kevlin looked around him. "So the question is, what's in the yard that's fast and seaworthy? That I can take out—and stay out in for a while? And fast enough to catch a racer?"

Tremain glanced at True, who nodded back.

"It's time to unveil our little surprise."

51

S PRAY FLYING off her bow, *Jolly Swagwoman* sliced through the waves, past the protective Sydney Heads, and dashed into the open reaches of the Tasman Sea.

Kevlin felt the vibration in the wheel as the big rudders bit deep. *Jolly Swagwoman* was doing 17 knots already, but she could do more.

He adjusted the Genoa and let out the main a bit. The knotmeter bumped up a knot, a satisfying reward.

This was the old boatbuilder's surprise.

Yes, it was that *Jolly Swagwoman*. Marci's boat was back, alive and well in his hands.

In fact, better than new, with re-engineered and carefully rebuilt parts, including a new specially reinforced bow, new keel, and new twin rudders.

The old boatbuilder had lavished all his skills in rebuilding Marci's beloved boat. She felt really solid in Kevlin's hands.

He cheerfully peered belowdecks. "How are we doing, crew?" There was a long silence.

He snapped on the automatic helm and sauntered below. True was at the nav station, struggling with the single sideband radio.

"Any contact, yet?" he inquired.

"Crappy reception," she answered. She had one hand to her head, and was slumped forward. A galvanized metal bucket was by her side.

"Probably some weather is sliding in," Kevlin said, "blocking reception."

He asked solicitously: "Is the seasickness medicine kicking in yet?"

"Nothing helps." She blanched white and shook her head.

She had been seasick the entire voyage so far, and showed no signs of getting well. It was normal to have some queasiness, or be sea sick for a short time.

But True was one of nature's unfortunates: she stayed sick.

The pills didn't help. They only seemed to make her groggy. Through it all, she gamely remained at her post, the bucket at her side.

"You insisted on coming," Kevlin felt obligated to point out.

"Thanks for reminding me." She lifted her head. "Any idea when we'll contact the first racers?"

"Not for a while," Kevlin said. "Can I get you something to eat..?"

"I don't think so."

"Maybe a little cheese..."

Too much.

Her face turned pale and she grabbed for the bucket.

52

TIME seemed to suspend itself. The sun set, the moon rose, the boat raced on.

Kevlin remained at the wheel to steer through the night, only going below to check on True and to make some coffee.

Toward dawn, he yawned, turned on the automatic pilot, then ambled below to get some sleep. It was his practice to stay at the helm during darkness, for safety's sake.

In his bunk, he tossed about, jostled by the racer, unable to fall sleep. Whenever he nodded off, thoughts of Marci came into his mind.

There was an odd little jolt to his nervous system and not an unpleasant one.

Hard to figure out exactly what it was. But it was definitely something.

It was as if *she* were here on the boat. *Her* boat. Getting into his mind.

He awoke, covered in sweat.

Marci was gone—he knew that.

But he found himself constantly looking about, as if he could turn his head quickly enough to discover her beside him.

Odd, he thought.

The sea does strange things to a tired mind.

*   *   *

By late morning, he had had enough. He slid off the bunk, got a cup of coffee from the thermos, then tried the radio, hoping the atmospheric interference had cleared enough to pick up a few signals from Sydney.

"Cheerio, lad," Tremaine's voice boomed. "How's she moving?"

"Like a homesick angel!" He glanced at his navigation readout, and gave his latest coordinates to Tremain. "We're doing 17 knots now," he added. "Overall, we've been averaging 14."

"Excellent. How's True holding up?"

"We're getting a lot of motion in these seas and she's still trying to adjust."

"That bad, eh?

"Not a happy sailor, but being brave. How soon do you make our intercept?"

"About eight hours—sunset," Tremain said.

"Heavy stuff is coming toward you now," he warned. "The weather bureau has updated the storm to a force 8 or 9. Winds gusting to 47 knots. A real buster."

He made his decision. "I'll keep pushing. Hard."

"You're not racing, you know."

"I need to reach the leaders before sunset. While I can still see something. Storm or no storm."

53

FLEXING HER MUSCLES, strengthening, she careened over the icebergs, leaping ever northward, vengeful. For her coming, winds jumped and began to moan. The seas began to build wildly into black towers.

The Lady was returning.

In her path lay the racers.

54

THE RACER SKITTERED nervously over the crests, then roared down the long slopes to bury her bow in a shower of spray. It was hard work to keep her moving smoothly between the growing mountains of water.

Kevlin was alone at the wheel, steering *Jolly Swagwoman* through the long Southern Ocean swells. The dark storm clouds to the south and west grew ominously on the horizon, their edges glowing a spectral red with the sunset.

Bad weather ahead. He squinted at the instruments: Unless the racers changed headings, he would run across their paths soon enough.

Maybe before the storm hit.

But where were they?

There was a scream of wind and the first unstable gusts hit. *Jolly Swagwoman* heeled in the blasts, buried her lee rail, and picked up more speed.

A blanket of fog swept around the speeding boat; the temperature plummeted.

The storm had arrived with rolling clouds of blankness.

Kevlin looked up in time to see the masthead vanish.

Moments later, the bow disappeared as well.

They were blind. The sweeping fog bank enfolded them and practically eliminated all vision.

55

THE BOAT would lurch, then wallow its way to the surface again. Water would race like it was out of a firehose down the deck, slamming into him in the cockpit.

He couldn't see ahead; steering was mostly guesswork. The fog patches cut his visibility to nothing.

If he overran a wave and didn't veer off, she'd roar down almost out of control and bury her nose in the back of the next. He felt the aft section of the giant racer lift, then ease back. It was like being on a kid's playground teeter-totter.

He raced into the teeth of the storm to find the racers—he could not bring himself to haul down sail.

In the storm, the radar couldn't pick out anything but high waves, spume and fog.

The racers could be anywhere.

*   *   *

He switched his radar down to short range to show any nearby danger. He tweaked the precipitation control to get a better return.

Still nothing.

The cold and the dankness of the fog bank was like a breath out of an open grave.

Kevlin strained his eyes at the phantom shapes that swirled toward *Jolly Swagwoman* in gray shrouds. What was that out there?

Another ship? Iceberg? No, just another fog bank.

Hold tight, folks. Grit teeth. Maintain course.

He swallowed hard, perspiration running into his eyes. His clothing clung to him under his foul weather gear. The sea was never hospitable.

Storms with fogs at night were always the worst.
He would be in for a long, hard night.

* * *

Ghostly waters. Kevlin clutched disconsolately at the wheel.
Nothingness amidst the sepulchral white fog. A bleakness
descended on him. He felt wet, cold, tired and terribly alone.
Suddenly, she was there.
She moved as if in a daze. Unsteadily, she pulled herself into
the wet cockpit.
"What can I do?"
Suddenly, he realized it was only True.
But there was something odd in her voice. Low, urgent.
Different. Kevlin could not quite make out what.
"Are you OK?"
"Sure. How can I help?"
"Be a lookout," he said. "Stay with me in the cockpit. We can't
even see the bow in this pea souper."
"Skipper, the bow's fifty feet ahead of you. Where's your hand-
held VHF radio?"
"What for?"
"On the bow, I'll have an advantage when we get to the top of
each crest."
"You'd get seasick again. In this weather...."
"...We could miss them. Or have a collision. With me up front,
at least we'll have a little more visibility."
"Crap. Even Marci wouldn't go up to the bow in this lousy
weather. "
"Yes, she would!" That was different.
Kevlin was startled as she continued: "Listen, just keep your
VHF turned up. If I see anything, I'll give you a holler."
She zipped up her foul-weather jacket, slicked back a hank of
blonde hair, then secured the hand-held with a stout lanyard
around her neck.
Satisfied, she clipped her safety harness onto the windward
lifeline, hunched forward and crawled forward out of the cockpit.
A fog bank rolled in. She seemed to pause in mid-deck, just

beyond the straining mast, turn back, wave and yell.

Her words, like the rest of her, was lost in the fog.

He thought she said, *"Ta, Luv."* Like Marci used to do.

Damn. Kevlin wondered if he was beginning to hallucinate.

*   *   *

Moments passed. Nervously, he yelled into his VHF. "Are you OK?"

The voice came eerily through the speaker. "Lousy visibility up here."

"Can you see anything out there?"

"Sure. Fog."

"Thanks for the update. Wait until the next wave crest. See if you can't spot something."

The big boat surfed down the back of one wave, skidded to one side, then climbed up another growler. At its crest, the bow reared high.

True cried: "Something over to port."

Kevlin scanned the horizon for anything that would show. A flash of color. A dark shadow in the white. Anything.

Suddenly, the narrow bow of a long green vessel materialized from the fog. A hank of jib, a huge mast, and then the Union Jack emblazoned on its side. Heywood Rand Garwood. *British Victory.*

The leading racer closed fast. Swaying in his cockpit, at the helm, Heywood stood to wave; the singlehander obviously surprised to see another human being. Kevlin and True waved back.

"Hello, chaps," came the English voice over the hand-held VHF radio. "Absolutely delighted. What the hell are you doing out here?"

"Looking for you. To warn you."

"Warn me? Good Lord. Against what?"

"We have reason to suspect..."

"What are you saying?"

From out of the fog, there was a thunderclap.

An explosion blossomed—and the English boat flew apart.

56

O N THE HIGH, jagged waves were scattered all that was left of the English racer: bits of fiberglass, a life preserver, some wreckage. These were tossed about, revealed only in the glimpses of the fog.

Lord Harwood was gone.

"What happened?" It was True on the radio.

"That was no accident," Kevlin yelled. "I'm heading over..."

"Watch out!" True yelled over the radio: "We've got company."

On the port bow, a lean shape slid out from the waiting fog bank, its color unmistakable.

Red.

"The *Satari*," True screamed.

Throwing the wheel over, Kevlin headed directly toward the intruder. *Jolly Swagwoman's* bow shot upward ten feet, then pounded in the growing waves.

The boat shuddered, then plunged ahead. The distance between the two racers decreased fast.

At the red boat's helm, a hooded figure gestured angrily and shouted something. The red boat veered off.

Blood began to pound in Kevlin's brain as *Jolly Swagwoman* slid by the *Satari's* red stern.

"Got him," Kevlin said. "We've got him red handed."

The apparition aboard the *Satari* turned, balancing a tube aboard its right shoulder.

Smoke erupted.

Something rocketed evilly toward *Jolly Swagwoman*.

57

THE WHEEL tore out of Kevlin's hand and he began a slow somersault backward. He could hear True screaming, even above the roar in his head. The water was like ice.

Then all was lost in a blur of white heat, noise and smoke.

*   *   *

He began to stir himself, his eyes focusing. The shock of the explosion was gone. Each breath he took brought on new chill.

God, it was so cold.

His body began to shake uncontrollably. The water was leaching away warmth from his body, and with it, his life.

How long had he been in the water? An minute? An hour? .

The seas battered him about, lifting and tossing him down the long route to the trough. At the bottom, he was encircled as if he were inside a huge green bottle.

Then he was carried up, up to the crest as the waves built again, until he was atop a surging emerald mountain.

The fog lay like a whirling shroud. He could see nothing beyond.

Where was True?

*   *   *

He shook his head, trying to clear his vision. He rubbed his eyes to clear the salt water.

Black.

He looked again: His hands were black from the explosion and bleeding. He couldn't feel his left leg. It hung limply below him in the water, trailing an ominously dark cloud.

Blood. Blood in the waters meant sharks.

Was *Jolly Swagwoman* still afloat? Probably sank like the Englishman's boat.

And the *Satari?*

* * *

His eyes scanned the horizon, between the waves. But all he could see was fog.

He was alone.

Between blood loss and sharks, he didn't figure he could last long. The shivering grew worse.

Something in the water bumped him. A hard object. Near his waist.

A hard rectangular-shaped object.

He held it aloft: it was the hand-held VHF radio he used to talk to True. Still on its lanyard around his neck.

He flicked the switch; a tiny diode gleamed red.

"Mayday, Mayday, Mayday!" He began transmitting. "This is the captain of *Jolly Swagwoman*. Our boat has sunk and we are in distress. I will talk to anyone within sound of my voice. Repeat, Mayday."

The hiss of static answered him.

He had a purpose. To transmit, and keep transmitting, as long as he could.

He'd stay alive as long as he did something. Anything.

Somewhere out there might be someone close enough to pick up the radio signals.

The shivering got worse.

58

SOMEWHERE IN THE FOG, the vessel changed course. The new bearing was displayed on his LED dial in the shape of a compass rose.

Little red lights blinked as the vessel took on a new heading. He could not—*must not*—fail again.

59

WHITECAPS CRASHED out of nowhere, plunging him down their sides into deep troughs—then elevated him up, up to the heights. Salt water stung his eyes, burned his face and seared his leg.

Kevlin desperately scanned the horizon, feeling himself beginning to lose consciousness in the bone-chilling water.

Where was the rescue ship?

In desperation, he held up the hand-held radio, turning up the volume. Only static blasted back.

He was absolutely alone. Despair descended on him like the oncoming darkness.

Don't lose focus, fall asleep and you'll never wake up, his mind whispered. His body was like lead; his legs were no longer his to control.

He slipped beneath the waves. A suicide sleep.

Choking, he sputtered back to the surface, inhaling gobs of air. He shook his head, hard, trying to clear it.

Then came the sound, a low wailing that shivered over the storm.

*   *   *

He raised his head above the water, turning his ears. Moments passed, but the cry was gone.

Instead there was the crashing of the waves, the howling of the wind.

Then it came again, softly, faint at first. It grew to an unearthly intensity. He strained his eyes toward the dark fog.

There was something in the distance.

A yellowish flickering light moved through the fog. Faint at first, then growing steadily brighter in hue and depth.

Yellow. Crimson.

And red.

A shiver ran through his body.

He refused to believe what his eyes told him.

Out of the dark, silhouetted in the flickering light, came a bloody angel.

Beckoning to him.

60

H E STOPPED SWIMMING, just treading water. The vision sent shivers up his spine, his mind unable to comprehend what his eyes told him.

The fog bank grew darker.

No sound came above the noise of the waves and the storm. Confused, doubting his senses, he began swimming again. Into the wind.

Toward the light.

*　　*　　*

It loomed in the darkness above him. He turned to face it, spinning wildly in the water.

She was riding low and heavy in the waves, in mortal agony, rising reluctantly to meet the waves, a shattered hulk, black with the explosion, like some giant beast had clawed out most of her top.

Her tall mast had a blackened mainsail; her tattered jib slatted in the wind, still smoking.

Kevlin desperately swam toward her, his breath coming in bursts. He grabbed the emergency ladder on the transom, then agonizingly heaved himself on board.

Jolly Swagwoman. She was somehow afloat. And *alive.*

In the storm, the motion of the boat was unnerving. Without speed to slice through the water, the racer plunged up, down and sideways.

Over the howl of the wind, something hammered mechanically, hurt down below: her bilge pumps were straining.

What was on the bow?

Wind and spray fought him as he inched his way forward. At the mast, he stopped, steadying himself and shielding his eyes against the storm.

The fog partly swept away, and in the ethereal light, the bow grew visible.

Icy fingers gripped his spine.

A body. It seemed to hover upright, its outline blurred and vague in the mists, as if surrounded by a milky shroud.

* * *

Spellbound, he moved forward with knees weak and stomach churning. He scarcely breathed.

Dear God, please. His blood felt like ice.

Her arms were spread-eagled, crucified in the lifelines and rigging. She swayed eerily with the pitch and roll of the racer.

The smoldering jib illuminated her silent agony in red. The blond head lifted slightly.

Hot emotion swept through his chest, his heart pounded. Unable to endure the sight, he broke the silence.

"True?" he yelled. "Oh, Lord, is it really you, Trudance!"

She seemed to shiver involuntarily, and her eyelids fluttered, then opened. She trembled, then somehow twisted her head around to face him.

He could scarcely breathe.

"God." He rushed past the smoldering jib, sawing desperately at the ropes with his knife. "Hang on. We'll get you out."

She fell helpless into his arms, and he pulled her back to the partially flooded cockpit area, trying to shelter her from the storm.

He held her head above the water, rubbing her wrists and ankles to restore circulation.

"I've been waiting for you." Her voice was a low, ragged whisper.

"You're going to be all right," he said, choking back tears.

He gently brushed a lock of golden hair from her forehead. His blackened fingers left smudges.

She settled against his chest and he felt the chill of her body. She stirred: "I thought I had lost you."

"Never going to happen!" he said, feeling hot emotion in his chest.

He felt himself starting to shiver; his face and blackened hands were hurting and his leg was getting numb. The explosion and his time in the water was catching up with him. He was beginning to weaken.

"Love you, True," he said, starting to slip away. He was in the arms of his private angel.

"Love you back. Always. Promise you'll never leave me."

"Promise," he said, grinning weakly. "And I keep my promises." He felt her arms squeeze him gently.

Involuntarily, his head turned.

He faced the sea once more.

*　　*　　*

Night was coming on. All he could make out were the crashing waves and dark fog. No horizon.

Beneath them, the racer gave a lurch and settled further into the water.

Kevlin muttered, "I don't know why this bucket is still afloat."

A gleam came to True's eyes, an odd light, but she said nothing.

She waited.

61

THE DIODES blinked red. His boat sliced through the waves, thrashing with the desperate speed it carried.

But he could not slow her now.

The instrument never varied, showing him the way ahead.

He had taken a blood vow.

No one could be left alive.

62

R ATTLING WITH SPEED, water exploding under its bow, the *Satari* closed in, her knife-like prow slicing toward them.

"It's going to hit us." True screamed.

Kevlin blinked open his eyes and peered through the fog to where she was pointing. He inhaled sharply.

But the *Satari* slashed past them, throwing seas off its powerful bow. It crested a wave, then disappeared.

Turning into the wind. Maneuvering.

True yelled. "He's got something in his hands."

A gleaming metal pipe. Recognition dawned. It was the rocket launcher.

*   *   *

Kevlin felt trapped. Adrenaline surged through his system; a hot flash of anger kicked in as he jumped toward the wheel. His blackened hands gripped the spokes.

"Hoist the mainsail." It seemed as if the ruined hulk shivered with purpose.

"You'll capsize us," True yelled. "We're too low in the water."

"Do it anyway."

Winches grated as the smoking mainsail hoisted, then hardened in the wind. *Jolly Swagwoman* lurched and moved ahead—slowly at first, then with growing conviction.

"What are you doing?" True screamed.

"Brace yourself!"

Kevlin clung to the shivering wheel.

There was life left in her; he could feel it. Somehow,

Swagwoman had come alive again. *Almost a supernatural presence.*

She moved faster now.

He whispered a prayer to the ruined racer and its last valiant effort.

*   *   *

Jolly Swagwoman caught a giant wave, picking up momentum all the way.

She was moving with a vengeance.

Directly ahead lay the other boat, lying abeam to the waves.

The red boat's skipper looked up from loading his launcher. Alarmed, he threw it down, desperately spinning the wheel, trying to turn his vessel.

There was a grinding, ripping sound as the hulk caught the red boat's carbon fiber hull, and punched through.

The collision gouged a large hole just below the water line, corkscrewing the red boat's bow down in the water. *Satari's* mast swayed like a willow branch, then cracked like a cannon under the pressure, buckling over the cockpit.

Somewhere beneath was the helmsman. He did not move.

True bounced against the cabin bulkhead; the force tore Kevlin from the wheel. He fell against True.

She was rigid with hate.

"Got him," snarled True in a voice he didn't recognize.

"Kill the bastard."

63

THE WAVES were horrific, lifting both boats together, then plunging them downward in a torrent of spray and twisting them about.

Satari's bow was riding low and heavy in the water; she was pilotless, in mortal agony.

Her mast was lying partly off the hull, but with broken chunks in the cockpit. The cockpit itself was a tangle of mast, lines and equipment.

Between lurches of the boat, Kevlin dashed forward to the bow of *Jolly Swagwoman*; it was like running on a bucking bronco. He stuck his head over the side, looking at the damage.

Jolly Swagwoman had struck hard; her reinforced bow remained deep in the red racer's forward side. They were locked together, pitched about by the waves.

And sinking.

Timing himself between the waves, he launched himself to the deck of the sinking racer.

*   *   *

A wave washed over him, but he grabbed a lifeline and crawled to the bow hatch, yanking it open.

In a torrent of water, Kevlin slid downward into darkness. He splashed about, felt bags, and determined he had landed in the sail locker.

Staggering, he slid open a bulkhead crash door and peered inside, blinking. Salt water stung his eyes; he wiped his face with a wet hand.

The forward compartment was lit with the eerie glow of the ship's running lights, and in the darkness below, one thing was clear. The racer's floor boards were awash.

He heard a high-pitched whine: her automatic pumps were on. But it was obvious she was taking on water faster than her pumps could throw it out.

From somewhere aft, above the racket of the grinding, came the noisy squawk of a high-powered radio. Behind a torrent of words the voice was familiar, but barely understandable. Kevlin only half-listened for a moment.

Blood roaring in his ears, his heart pounding, Kevlin stumbled forward in the plunging bow.

The water was up to his waist.

*   *   *

Ahead of him, groaning as if it were alive, *Jolly Swagwoman's* battered bow shivered back and forth in the waves, grinding away at the red racer's hull, enlarging the hole.

Jolly Swagwoman was jammed about four feet into the racer's side, green water spurting in.

Shards of carbon fiber, like long black knives, cracked from the *Satari's* sides and lay splintered about.

Beneath him, the broken boat groaned, grinding against its broken spine.

Satari was sinking.

When she went under, she would drag the ruined *Jolly Swagwoman* down with her.

His breathing was coming quick and hard.

If he could somehow shove *Swagwoman's* bow back out, he and True would at least have a boat under them. That might save them.

With a lever, he could try to pry the two giants apart between the waves.

*   *   *

He looked about, desperately. In the corner of the bow, he saw it: a spare spinnaker pole.

He levered it into position and shoved hard.

Green water gushed in.

The boat lurched, the bow shot skyward and came down with a boom and a grinding noise.

The boats were still locked together.

Something hummed in the air beside his head.

*   *   *

Kevlin fell into the dark water, twisting on his injured leg.

A shadowy creature crouched above him, eyes glittering with hate. In its hands, it held some sort of black club.

The first swing had missed.

The second wouldn't.

Satari was dying.

But her skipper was very much alive.

64

K EVLIN'S HANDS searched underwater frantically for a weapon; anything. His fingers closed on a carbon fiber shard. Sharp, like a knife

Sakko moved forward. "Try to understand—nothing personal." His eyes became cold and focused.

Sakko lunged with terrible ferocity, intending to kick him to death.

He was smiling, deliberate and sure in his attack. He knew how to do this.

Sakko's eyes opened wide in pain. And revelation.

The carbon spear slammed into Sakko's mid-section, the force of his rush jamming it deep.

"No," he cried, desperately.

He lurched forward, then slipped to his knees.

The spear caught in the floorboard, inching toward the heart, the pain nearly overwhelming him.

He fell backwards into the water.

Sakko raised his head, his eyes questioning.

"Better you than me, Sakko."

*   *   *

With great effort, the warrior clutched a bulkhead and raised himself. His eyes glittered with fury.

There was very little time left. Kevlin had to know.

"All those senseless killings," Kevlin accused. "All for the sake of a race."

"Race?" Sakko grunted with pain. "Don't play such an innocent."

"What is this shit?"

"We were on to you."

"I don't get that."

"Come on! We had to get your agent, Bruce. The foundry worker was with him when I arrived. I could take no chances... both numbers had to go."

"Numbers? But....Marci? For chrissakes. Did you have to kill her?"

"If we could have dropped the keel, and left the boat intact, we would have done so."

"You were only after the keel...?"

Sakko gasped, blood oozing form the corner of his mouth.

He was visibly weakening.

Kelvin came closer, trying to hear. "Inside the keel?"

"...the keels...with the depleted plutonium ballast."

Sakko was making a visible effort now to get his words out. "It had to be in one of the four plutonium keels, Marci, New Zealand, France....and

"...Lord Harwood's boat."

*   *   *

"I got them all," Sakko's eyes shone in triumph. "You lose."

"You're crazy."

"We saved lives, old sport," Sakko gasped. "Four lives gone... but hundreds of thousands saved. Big numbers."

"Saved lives?" Kevlin visibly paled.

Sakko half raised himself out of the water and turned his agonized face toward Kevlin.

"You might as well admit it. I'm not the bad guy. *You are.*"

65

THE *SATARI* LURCHED again, groaning, its angle increasing. There was a grinding, ripping noise as *Jolly Swagwoman's* reinforced bow bit deeper into the ruined racer.

No question—they were going down.

Sakko managed a glance at the blocked hatchway. "Ironic. We're both trapped. "

"Not yet, Sakko."

Kevlin painfully raised himself, moving forward in the waist deep water on the tilting cabin floor, feeling his way about in the eerie emergency red lights.

Sakko was still talking. Kevlin could make only snatches above the groaning of the dying boat and the noise of the storm.

Forward. Toward the grinding.

If he could not get out, at least he could free *Jolly Swagwoman.* That would save True.

*   *   *

Sakko, now barely holding himself up, beckoned Kevlin nearer.

"A white phosphorous device," Sakko said, almost offhand.

"Keep going. I'm listening." Kevlin kept moving, trying to concentrate.

"Underwater....I attached a roll...around...keel."

Kevlin stopped.

"Detonator... was a mercury switch. CIA used them..for car bombs. Motion comes...mercury electric contact...and boom!"

"...Motion? Such as a storm? And the keel gets blown off."

"No. No bomb." Sakko stared ahead stoically. "Carbon fiber...

has tragic weakness. Melts."

Yeah. Kevlin was listening hard. Here it was, all coming out—now that they both were dying. Going down together in the boat.

"Heat," Kevlin said, "like an acetylene torch. A ring of heat severs the keel. And off it drops."

"Too obvious, old sport." Sakko's eyes glittered.

The game was taking his mind off the shock and pain. "And too easily detected. Try this: Keel melts only part way. Weakens. Big wave....breaks it. Crack...over goes the racer."

He permitted himself a thin smile.

"The others? The Frenchman. The broken Kiwi rudder?"

"Same. A storm....boat rocks...device goes off. Keel or rudder is cut part way."

"Then it breaks."

"And not detectable."

"The heat ring....caused the outer parts to melt and be smooth. And the break itself...sharp parts."

That was the key: he had not fully understand why the outer layer was smooth and melted; he had concerned himself only at sharp parts. It means failure under stress.

Wow. So there it was. So obvious he had overlooked it.

"Here's the big one, Sakko. Why? Why did you do it?"

"Spent plutonium...," he managed to gasp. "...bomb."

"Hold it! You're hallucinating."

"No joke. Bomb."

Sakko began gasping. His eyelids fluttered. "*Sid...*" Sakko said urgently.

"Who's he? Sakko, I don't have time..."

"....watch out...for Sid...."

"Sid who?" Kevlin yelled. "Sid who? You're losing me."

"...unfinished...."

* * *

Sakko slumped forward, his dying body quivered, the light went out of his eyes. His body sketched out, face down in the water.

"Sakko..." Kevlin cried, pulling him out. He felt the neck vein for a pulse and looked into his sightless eyes.

Sakko was dead.

And Kevlin would follow.

*   *   *

Time was against him. He had to move quickly, do something.

He dragged himself forward as fast as he could. Inside the forward compartment, the bow was low in the water.

Swagwoman was jammed in, her battered bow groaning as waves slammed the two boats together.

Salt water spray blasted in, hurting his eyes and fouling his vision.

He felt dark waters grow deeper around him, creeping up toward his head.

He began to go down.

66

WITH TERRIBLE groaning noises, *Swagwoman* was grinding away at the side of the hull.

Desperately, Kevlin crawled forward to the bow area, bracing himself between waves.

The water was growing higher.

"True," he yelled. "I'm trapped."

Only the broken noises of the two ruined racers came back over the storm's noise.

He moved close to the holed area: *Satari* was doomed, her keel broken. Every wave that came along ground the two boats together. But the hole was enlarging at the top, not the bottom.

Floatation bulkheads. Some of *Swagwoman's* bulkheads had remained somehow intact in her reinforced bow and these were holding her up; the *Satari* was slowly dragging her down.

In the darkness, the water level had grown higher; Kevlin felt its chill up to his chin. He shielded his eyes from the spray of the collision area.

Leverage was what he needed. Fumbling around Sakko's floating body, he nearly missed it: a spare spinnaker pole.

He jammed the long pole into the collision area and put all his weight on it. He grunted, then jammed again.

The pole snapped; carbon fiber shards flew. The leverage was too much for the pole and he fell back into the waves, his energy at last exhausted.

He floated in the water, doomed. He could not help but turn to stare at the body, lying face up in the water. Moved by inner currents. Sakko's arms were waving, up and down.

As if beckoning Kevlin to join him.

67

K EVLIN ROLLED over on his back and stared numbly at the blocked bow hatch, so tantalizingly close. It hovered above him in a murky luminescence.

He pushed and shoved, but the hatch was pinned down by the broken mast and the tangled of rigging. He could not free it. Nor could he free *Swagwoman* before the mortally broken racer he was trapped in dragged his own boat down.

"Think, dammit think," he commanded himself.

What was it that Sakko said—about heat?

Splashing through the water, he charged into the depths of the hull, searching desperately until he came to the galley. He stood very still, squinting his eyes in the eerie darkness feeling with his outstretched hand. Here was where Sakko had prepared his meals.

And here lay not one, but two single burner butane galley stoves, with their small canisters of gas underneath. He stood only for a moment, panting with his exertions. His heartbeat quickened. He knew them well. He had a similar stove on his own boat.

The stoves were in reality little kitchen blowtorches, quickly heating up coffee and food. They had their own sparking lighter in them. Sakko had the best.

Racing now, Kevlin grabbed the two stoves, one in each hand, and plunged forward, sliding crazily through the water to the bow.

He turned on one stove's gas, twisted the ignition dial to light it; the stove hesitated, sputtered, then began to roar. The bright flame hurt his eyes; he felt the heat in his hand as he lifted the tiny stove above him and directed the blue flame to the *Satari's* hull. Smoking and smelling of burning epoxy, the carbon fiber oozed in black gobs. The flame cut deeper.

And then....a ray of light. A whiff of fresh sea air.

Yes. He had cut through the hull's thickness. Grinning wildly, he ignited the other stove, and turned both up to full power. Their blue blames seared at the hull, melting it in a giant arc starting where *Swagwoman's* bow had jammed in.

Drops of melted carbon fell sputtering into the dark waters as he enlarged the hull area. Scattered bits of fiery debris splattered like fireworks, falling to icy waters, nearly chin high.

With a grating noise, the *Satari's* bow began to move. It seemed to bend away from the cut, trembling with the pressure of the waves. Kevlin felt the power, gritted his teeth and worked harder with his torches. Underneath him the boat began to vibrate.

A cracking sound— he glanced up from his work. Water surged into the hole as the last of the *Satari's* crash bulkheads burst.

Two things seemed to happen at once: *Swagwoman's* bow lifted away and Kevlin was slammed backwards into the darkness with the surge. He was flailing, groping, hoping for a hold. Anything.

He carried one grateful thought with him: *Swagwoman* was free. He had saved True.

* * *

The *Satari* gave a shudder and groaned as it rolled to one side, then rose nearly vertical, air compressing inside the long hull, weighted down by onrushing water and tons of keel ballast.

Kevlin grabbed the cockpit hatch, pounded his fists, and then slammed his knees at it.

In its death throes, the *Satari* jarred her broken mast to one side. The hatch burst open.

Free! In a burst of air bubbles, Kevlin was out.

He watched as the stern of the *Satari* slid below him. Into the depths. Forever. Gasping, he was on the surface. A dark shape was near.

With failing strength, he swam toward it and felt hands gripping his collar.

68

IN THE *Swagwoman's* partly flooded cockpit, True cradled Kevlin's head in her lap, consoling him.

"Don't leave me," she said, over and over. Her hands came away bright with blood where she held him.

He managed to open his eyes. "I'm still here."

She was silent as she stared at him.

Finally: "What I care about is you."

"True," he squeezed her arm.

"I thought I'd lost you."

"Yeah, I thought I was a goner, too. Sakko didn't help."

"Sakko?"

"He was below. And he...killed them all." His voice shook.

"What?"

"He told me before he died. And something weird..."

He was about to say more, then gasped as something seemed to tear inside and his arm fell limply in the cockpit's water.

"Kevlin?" True called desperately. "Don't go."

She clutched him to her, blood all over her clothing.

She was suddenly, terribly alone.

69

THE SKY to the east seemed to brighten as if a star had loosened itself from the heavens and began heading toward them.

A vibrating roar filled the sky, followed by the whump-whump-whump of giant blades.

A searchlight pierced the blackness.

"Ahoy, *Swagwoman.*"

True waved feebly.

The giant helicopter poured blasts of air down on them. A voice boomed: "We're lowering a safety harness."

Kevlin blinked in the bright light, trying to raise himself in the near swamped cockpit. True had to help him into the harness.

She motioned for the crew to take up the slack, his harness jerked and the deck fell away beneath him. Strong hands grabbed him out of the blast of the rotors and pulled him inside.

Kevlin leaned his dazed head against the helicopter's window. "Oh, my god," he uttered.

Far below, as True was hoisted, *Swagwoman's* bow began to disappear in the waves.

The water rolled unobstructed up the deck and into the cockpit. She lifted her stern for a brief moment, then tipped her mast forward as in a final salute.

In the space of a heartbeat, she slipped quietly into the dark seas.

And then she was gone.

*   *   *

Someone put a blanket around his shivering shoulders; another uniformed flyer poured hot tea from a thermos.

True joined him.

A sergeant asked: "Are there more survivors down there?"

Kevlin shook his head. "No."

The sergeant said something over the intercom and powerful engines roared. The chopper lifted away from the water and swung to a new bearing.

"How'd you find us?" Kevlin managed to ask.

"We were steaming to your general coordinates when our bridge picked up your distress call."

"Bridge? You're from a ship?"

"Coast Guard, sir. Our vessel was alerted when you missed your radio contact with home base. We tracked your sailboat with radio bearings and infrared..."

True lifted her head.

The crewman took a deep breath. "...and as we homed in, well, let me say there was something odd. Something about your boat."

He hesitated. "But we all saw it. ..a soft glow. Probably just phosphorescence..."

His voice trailed off.

"Otherwise I can't explain it."

True nodded, then looked away.

She knew.

SECTION
FOUR

DEATH
ON THE
WIND

70

T HE TELEVISION set woke him. He opened his eyes, bleary with too much sleep.

He'd been in the hospital for days, make that weeks. Private room. He had lost count of time, but the bandages on his hands were light gauze now, not the heavy tan velcro. He had pretty much healed up and he was getting his strength and energy back.

There was a burst of music and a long shot of a sailboat was coming into Sydney harbor.

The cops kept the TV on so that the one on duty at his bedside could pass the time. Whether Kevlin wanted it or not.

Or maybe just to keep the cop awake. The officer was middle aged and with a bulge over his heavy police belt. He overate and he had a tendency to doze off. And snore.

*   *   *

Kevlin focussed on the TV set. "*Solo Eagle* is arriving," the announcer was excitedly saying. "Up from the Furious Fifties and Roaring Forties, and a great adventure, this is the incredible leading vessel in the Race Alone Around the World. With an amazing rescue to its credit."

A telephoto shot showed Corky Bowman in the cockpit, waving wildly to the cheering crowds.

"Next to him is the New Zealand racer, Sidney Wellington, whose *Black Magic Flyer* was encircled by ice. The subject of Bowman's heroic rescue."

There was a shot panning the harbor, showing many boats of various kinds flying flags, people waving madly, giving the skippers a royal welcome.

A quick closeup of the boat, a zoom in to Bowman and

Wellington, followed by a superimposed series of shots taken earlier of the racer under construction.

Flashback. There was Corky, a sanding grinder in his hand, beside the transom. Corky in the cockpit, fiberglassing in a section. Corky with his lopsided grin, and boyish charm, marred only by the almost pirate-like scar that extended from his left temple down to his cheek.

Then the music came up wildly as the boat sailed out of the harbor.

Cut back to present time, live: the boat, surrounded by enthusiastic well-wishers.

*   *   *

"We're going on board this amazing racer in a few minutes," the jubilant announcer continued, but to Kevlin the words began to blur.

Sweat stood out on his brow as he desperately tried to figure out what was happening.

The TV shots stirred up memories.

He felt at some detached level that he was on the brink of discovery—one that would unlock the rest of a mystery.

An epiphany.

If he could just summon the energy to put it all together.

71

THE TV COVERAGE was superb. Bands played, banners fluttered, and applause rang through the air as the big wooden sloop tied up at the end of the pier, her tall mast spearing the sky in easy circles.

The pitiless cameras exposed her scarred hull—there was no doubt she had been sailed hard—down in the Roaring Forties, the Furious Fifties, and for a brief dash, into the Screaming Sixties. That was the shortest route, but it was not for naught it was also called the Suicide Sixties.

What a boat. The Sydney crowd, keenly appreciative of sailing craft and bold sailors, clapped wildly. Small children oohed and ahhed in glee. Flags flew.

*   *   *

Sweating in his hospital bed, Kevlin saw thousands of well-wishers and a flock of newspeople greeting Corky Bowman and Sidney Wellington.

A panning shot showed *Solo Eagle* tying up at the pier and a voice-over intoned the details of the race. The cameras picked out every detail of the solo sailors being spirited away to a raised platform near the center of the pier.

The welcoming ceremony got into full swing.

"We welcome these brave lads to our shores..." the mayor of Sydney intoned as the crowd took up the chant, *"Syd..ney! Syd..ney!"*

Kevlin's focus was drawn to Corky.

He stood quietly to one side, still dressed in his salt-stained foul-weather gear. His boyish looks were only enhanced by his dark beard and his livid scar.

He flashed a smile to the appreciative crowd.

"Yey, Sydney!" Corky gave them the high sign. "Right back at you."

The crowd went wild with applause.

*   *   *

Perspiring heavily, Kevlin threw back the covers and sat slowly up in bed. He felt well enough but his memory was only painfully sliding back. He was beginning to connect up pieces of the puzzle.

What was it?

The cop glanced up: "Easy there, mate."

"Urgent," Kevlin said, swinging his feet over the sides. Reeling, he glanced at the bedside mirror and winced. His beard had grown since the time he last put to sea and was thick, dark and bushy.

His hair was long—practically shoulder length. His eyes were sunken and dark.

He leaned down, as if to breathe deeply, then straightened up, still tangled in his sweaty bedsheets. He held something in his right hand.

The fat cop rose from his chair. "Want to go to the loo? Use the bedpan. That's why it's there, mate."

"To the harbor."

The cop looked disgustedly at his charge. "Forget it."

"Important."

Sensing trouble, the uniformed policeman stepped forward to shove Kevlin back into his sickbed, grabbing one of the leather bedside restraints used for prisoners.

He wrestled Kevlin's arm into position and was wrapping the heavy leather strap around his wrist when he saw a blur of motion.

There was a metallic whack as Kevlin brought down the bedpan on the uniform's head. He wilted to the floor, unconscious.

"Sorry, mate," Kevlin muttered as he looked wildly about. He was still in his hospital gown. The cops had taken his clothing.

*   *   *

He dashed into the next room, and to the astounded gaze of the bed-patient, ran to the closet and grabbed his clothing.

"Hey! the patient yelled. "Them are mine. Where do you think you're going?"

"Out," said Kevlin, slipping on oversized, baggy black pair of trousers, floppy khaki-colored shirt, and scuffed white shoes.

Standing up, Kevlin had to grab for the pants to keep them from falling down. They no longer had a crease, and had stains of food, and possibly, booze on them.

"Them are my pants. What're you gonna do?"

"Nothin."

"Yeah, well. Hoist one for me, mate." The patient rolled over and closed his eyes.

Kevlin obviously was making a break for a beer. And not a bad idea at that.

Kevlin peered into the hallway. It was clear except for the nurse station at the end of the corridor. No one looked up. The cop on duty had not yet recovered consciousness.

In his flopping shoes, Kevlin unsteadily tiptoed down the corridor.

An elevator light flashed on, indicating someone was getting off at this floor.

He tried to hurry to the nearby door to the stairwell—and freedom—and managed to duck inside just as two hospital maintenance workers got off.

He paused only momentarily to wipe the sweat from his eyes with the back of his hand, then steadied himself on the rail as he took the steps slowly, one at a time.

It was painful taking the steps.

On the ground floor, he forced himself into a shaky trot, past the parked cars, heading for the nearby waterfront.

Something he had *heard* lodged in his memory.

Instinct was kicking in.

He had to hurry.

72

KEVLIN LOPED along side streets and alleys, heading down to the waterfront. His clothes flapped in the strong breeze; the effect made him look like a scarecrow.

But he had no time to worry about his appearance.

A police car, red light flashing drifted by. He shrunk into a doorway, his heart hammering.

The route was simple: downhill. Everything in Sydney led to the water, and so long as Kevlin stumbled down, he knew he was headed in the right direction.

There was also the hubbub. The ceremonies were in full swing, complete with a mass choral arrangement, the crowd cheering wildly and yacht's horns and whistles going off.

The problem was that time had become suddenly precious. He had the sense that the clock was running out. On him. And something else he couldn't quite bring up to the surface of his memory. Quite yet.

He slunk through the shadows, from alley to alley. In this part of Sydney, no one paid any attention to him: obviously, he was just another rough-hewn waterfront wino in search of his next slug of booze or drug hit.

He came to the end of a tangled, brick-covered alley; below him lay the vista of the harbor. Down the pier lay the scarred and dented sailboat that had fought its way around the world.

Between it and him were the crowds, in an appreciative mood, an island nation showering its favor on a man with the scar who had conquered the oceans of the world—and saved a fellow sailor from certain death in the icy reaches of the Southern Ocean.

His heart pounded wildly as he lurched forward.

73

THE DISHEVELED MADMAN in the flapping clothing fought his way through the crowds and headed toward the speakers.

A startled mayor looked up, mouth agape, from his microphone. He pointed his finger at the wild man shoving his way through the crowds.

"Danger." Kevlin panted, nearing the raised platform.

"What is this nonsense?" Corky Bowman stepped forward, glaring at Kevlin.

A councilman beside him shook his head angrily. "Just another anti-nuke demonstrator."

"Try to understand," Kevlin yelled. *"Here."*

As soon as he spoke he realized that his warning must have sounded absurd.

He turned wildly, his clothes flapping in the harbor breeze like a scarecrow's, and pointed his outstretched finger toward the end of the pier.

"Danger!"

"What's that weirdo yapping about?" snapped Corky, suddenly alert. He scowled.

The newspeople clicked their cameras; TV cameras focused on the disturbance.

"Police!" Someone yelled. "Get the loony out of here!"

Kevlin felt deep despair. He realized he wasn't making sense to the crowd. Or to the officials.

In fact, he could not explain it to himself.

*   *   *

Siren blaring, a police car came roaring down the pier. Three uniformed cops poured out, running for Kevlin.

"Hold on," Kevlin yelled. "Please. I'm trying to help."

The mayor called out to the police: "Says he needs help."

Someone replied, with a broad Aussie accent: "They'll give it to him. Lots of help."

More laughter. Louder jeers.

"Take the loony away," someone yelled over the PA system.

The police closed in to a wildly gesturing Kevlin.

*   *   *

He looked desperately about; he was hemmed in on all sides. He found himself being jerked away, jostled through the crowd.

A bearded paparazzi elbowed himself in front of Kevlin and his police escorts, raising his camera to get his shot.

One policeman stumbled off balance, then swore.

Kevlin shoved the other cop, then broke loose to the pier's edge.

He put on a sudden burst of speed and the waters rushed up to greet him.

He hit the surface with a hollow boom of water and disappeared in the depths.

74

DARK SHADOWS lay under the pier as Kevlin surfaced. The dive to the water had been a long one, and it left Kevlin hurting from the impact.

His face stung, but he was still lucky: no one had followed him into the water.

The black pilings and dark shadows were on Kevlin's side. He had camouflage protect him, at least for a little while, as he swam further out to the end.

Behind him, the sounds of the crowd faded. They had lost interest in him. He was aware of muffled voices and rhythmic cadences on the PA system.

Some announcement, then, hurriedly music.

The ceremony was back in full bore again—probably wrapping up.

He made his way past two cruising boats and a yacht, all empty—their sailors apparently at the ceremony. Hurry. Kevlin rapidly swam toward the end of the pier— and what lay there.

A large, scarred hull loomed indistinctly in the shadows.

*   *   *

He stayed in the quiet dark of the pier, glanced furtively about. He had to be certain he wasn't seen.

Taking a final gulp of air, Kevlin dived deep, following the lines of her bilge down, down farther than he had originally imagined.

There was a heavy keel tapering from the hull.

At the very bottom, in the darkening depths nearly twenty feet below, lay the ballast bulb.

It loomed huge in the water like an oversized torpedo, scarred and dented from its passage through the storms and ice, its bottom paint nearly scratched away.

He came up. Dripping water and oily harbor ooze, he emerged at the stern and shakily clambered aboard the boat's transom. He shivered in the harbor breeze, flapped his arms to his sides to warm himself in the sunlight.

He caught himself in mid-stretch. He had to keep moving—not get nabbed again.

Kevlin was perspiring heavily now. He knew that he was not thinking straight.

He staggered across the cockpit, past the oversized steering wheel, and shoved at the hatch cover. It was unlocked.

In his hurry with the dockside ceremonies, Corky had walked off and left it open.

Kevlin quickly disappeared below, running on instinct. What was he looking for—exactly?

He began his search at the bow, glanced through the forepeak and the bags of sails, then proceeded to the stern. Everything was in its place. *Nothing. Wrong.*

More applause and cheering drifted down through an open hatch from the wrapup of the ceremonies. From somewhere came the wail of sirens.

The net was closing; soon they'd have divers in the water, checking for him or his body.

He didn't have anything to show for his efforts—or much time left.

*   *   *

Disgusted, Kevlin slumped on the cabin's floorboards.

It was stifling hot inside the boat; sweat poured from him and his bandaged hands itched.

Was he going mad? Was it the hospital medications that made him act so? He felt out of control, running like a bullet spinning to its target.

He was about to give up, and quietly surrender, when cool air drifted up and teased his sweaty brow.

From where? Below. He lifted the floorboards and peered into the bilge of the racer. He bent down, inserting his head into the darkness, looking forward.

Nothing.

He gently lifted up another floorboard and looked below at the heavily-built keel area.

Normal. Nothing out of the ordinary.

Time to give it up.

*   *   *

Then he saw it. It was nearly invisible, a black wire in the darkness, the thick, waterproof kind. It led through a special fitting into the keel, disappearing below.

Kevlin studied the wire for a few moments, then touched it. If one end led downward, where did the other go? What did it do?

The analytical part of his mind worked overtime. He let his fingers follow the wire back from the keel area along the stringers, past the frames, to an area below the cockpit. Odd.

He lifted up more floorboards, laying them to one side.

It exited somewhere below the cockpit.

A single wire.

Kevlin poked his head out of the entryway. There was the usual assortment of GPS and other devices necessary to navigate and monitor a vessel on the steering pedestal, near the wheel. But where did the single black wire lead?

Frustrated with uncertainty, he tugged lightly, and the wire lifted free off the bottom. He held it between his fingers, tracing it to a small, nearly invisible panel.

His fingers felt around the heavily built wooden panel. There. A hidden switch in the framing released a small trapdoor.

Inside was a black box with a digital display.

Red letters glowed: *2 hours, 37 minutes, and 43 seconds. Then 42 seconds. Now 41. A countdown of some sort.*

One red diode was lit.

It said: *Armed.*

75

THE RED DIGITAL DISPLAY kept changing. *Two hours, 35 minutes, and 10 seconds.*

Kevlin's feverish mind raced as the fog over his memory started burning away.

He was back on board the sinking red racer now, and in front of him was a dying madman, boasting that he'd gotten them all.

But he had warned, *"Sid."*

It wasn't a man's name at all. It was what the crowds on the pierheads were shouting,

Phonetically. *"Sid."*

Could it be? "*Sid.* As in *"Sydney?"*

Danger.

It was here. Below him.

Horror shook through him. In an oversized keel ballast bulb, not of spent plutonium, but of hollow lead. A bulb that was big enough to contain a very *special* kind of bomb.

Undetectable.

Two hours, 29 minutes and 45 seconds.

All the time that was left for Sydney Harbor.

All that remained for Sydney.

76

NO TIME LEFT. Kevlin dropped to his stomach and tugged at the wire; it wouldn't budge from the keel. He moved back to the control panel.

One hour, 17 minutes, 45 seconds.

Seizing a heavy diver's knife from beside the hatchway, he slammed the heavy blade into the wire, and began sawing at it. It only dented the outer casing.

Stop. He halted his work, perspiration rolling off his face.

What was he doing?

Even the simplest terrorist devices had a fail-safe.

If the counter should stop, or the wire was severed between the timer and the bomb, a trigger would trip.

Setting off the bomb.

He wasn't a demolition expert, but he knew he was in trouble.

The knife dropped, clattering in the bilge. Useless.

One hour, 15 minutes.

And ticking.

77

C ORKY Bowman fidgeted during the ceremony and perspired heavily, despite a brisk harbor wind.

He glanced at his watch. *Damn.*

"Sir," he said in an urgent voice to the mayor, "I'm feeling a little woozy— I must not have my land legs yet."

As the welcoming committee gave him a worried look, he covered his mouth with his hand. He cleared his throat.

The mayor got the message. He didn't want the hero of the hour to vomit on the ceremonies—in full display of the TV cameras—and quickly intoned:

"Let's give a big Sydney welcome to Corky Bowman, who has to leave us now."

Applause rattled the pier as Corky made his way down the steps and past the crowds.

Police vehicles had cordoned off the pier's end, their red lights flashing, as divers searched under the piers for the madman who had interrupted the ceremony.

Behind him he could hear the mayor continuing his welcome, this time concentrating his attention on Sid Wellington.

Bowman began to lope down the pier past the assembled boats. Sweat rolled off him in increasing waves. *Hurry.*

There wasn't much time left.

He stopped short as he neared the end of the pier.

His boat was gone.

78

ONE HOUR, 14 minutes. And counting. So far, the end of the pier was still quiet, cordoned off by the ceremony. Police vans and cars held back the crowd.

Under the pier, among the pilings, the divers were working methodically underwater.

And coming nearer.

Time was ticking away —and so was Sydney's life.

The wind was out of the west, blowing gustily. *Solo Eagle* was just barely docked—still ready to fly.

Kevlin quickly uncleated the mooring lines and the racer slid easily away from the pier.

"Hey, she's moving!" Someone from the distance shouted over the widening gap. Startled heads in the crowd turned to stare at him.

He jerked the mainsail aloft. The big boat heeled with the wind's power and Kevlin jumped to the steering wheel. Adrenaline was pumping hard now, giving him the energy to move.

She was quick, this one.

No time to set the jib—he didn't need that for what he wanted. He quickly guided the racer out to the harbor's entryway, dodging other boats.

Hurry.

Long waves greeted him and spray whipped across his face as he raced toward the huge Sydney Heads that protected the beautiful harbor.

Ahead lay the Tasman Sea—and hope.

*   *   *

The wind seemed to double as he neared open water; the boat

heeled sharply and dug in.

From above him came the clatter of a helicopter. An electronic voice commanded: "Stop and prepare to be boarded." The police had found him.

The helicopter hovered menacingly nearer, its blades edging close to the vessel's mast.

Kevlin waved his arms frantically, trying to motion the helicopter to go away. He saw the pilot talking on his headset and a uniformed cop in the passenger side lift a long-range rifle, aiming it at him.

Without warning, the helicopter veered off. In moments, Kevlin saw why.

A high-speed boat screamed in the distance. A cigarette boat, the high-powered craft used for offshore races.

As it closed, Corky Bowman waved his fist and shouted, "You stole my boat, asshole!"

"I know what you've got on board."

"We need to talk. *Really* talk."

Maybe there was a way to stop this madness. "Come alongside," Kevlin shouted warily.

It was a chance he had to take.

Corky expertly maneuvered the large motorboat abeam. Kevlin threw him a line; Corky made it fast, and scrambled on board.

"The bomb." Kevlin confronted him: "What the hell are you doing?"

"Get off it," Corky seemed mildly amused. "That must be pretty strong stuff you've been getting at the hospital."

"The red dial below. I found it."

"Oh, that? That's my control panel for photovoltaic cells. You fucked that one up, old buddy."

Corky shouldered his way past Kevlin.

"What're you doing?"

"Just going below. To collect my gear. Passports, money, clothes—stuff I need on shore."

Corky was at the companionway, one arm holding something at his side.

"Bullshit." Kevlin charged at Corky, caught him in the midriff with a football block. Corky went backward down the companionway, took a header and fell heavily against the cabin floor. A belaying pin bounced from his hand.

Kevlin slammed the hatch shut, locking it. Kevlin was in the cockpit while Corky raged below.

"Let me out of here!" Corky pounded his fists.

"Turn the sonofabitch off."

Silence. Then, "Go fuck yourself."

*   *   *

Salt spray greeted him as the boat passed the giant Heads and entered the open waters of the Tasman Sea. Kevlin thumped his hand on the hatch. "Still down there?"

No answer.

Kevlin perspired heavily. His plan wasn't working. Time was ticking away.

Rummaging beneath the cockpit tool lockers, Kevlin found what he was looking for. A heavy fireman's ax.

He snapped the autopilot on so the racing craft would hold its course and then he moved forward toward the bow. The going was wet, the foredeck slippery with foam and water.

Timing between waves, he hoisted the ax over his head and brought it down onto the racer's side, near the bow area.

With a sickening thud, the sharp blade easily cut deep into the hull's laminated wood. As the bow dipped under a wave, water slipped into the hole.

"Hey!" Corky yelled, now very alert. "What the fuck are you doing?"

"Tick. Tick. Tick. Got something you need to do?"

No answer. Kevlin worked the ax up and down the sides of the bow several more times. As each wave struck, the sea flooded below.

"Asshole! You're sinking us."

"Think fast. You don't have much time."

From below came a high pitched mechanical whine. Corky had turned on the emergency bilge pumps.

Beneath his feet, Kevlin could feel the bow shiver and sink a little in the waves. Some water was being forced out, but not nearly enough. The pumps couldn't keep up.

Kevlin made his way back to the cockpit and adjusted *Solo Eagle*'s course a few degrees starboard of dead downwind; white water roiled over the foredeck and gunwales. He levered open the cockpit's wooden floor to expose the steering mechanism. He found what he was looking for and slammed the ax home.

He turned to the mainsheet, letting it out until the booming sail was caught bar-taut in the force of the westerly.

Eagle was roaring.

The bow sliced into a wave. Green water ran back over the foredeck, lapping greedily. *Eagle*'s nose dropped markedly lower.

"Bastard...she's *going.*" It was Corky.

The wind tore at the sinking vessel, now fighting for stability as well as buoyancy. Waves smashed along the sinking bow, pouring firehose pressure jets of water below. Green water tore back toward the cockpit. Foaming white, a wave noisily overran them.

"*No...*" screamed Corky, his voice hoarse. "I'm trapped."

"One last chance," Kevlin said, thumping the boat's side with the ax. "Is that thing below what I think it is?"

A moment of silence, then an angry: *"Yes."* And louder, *"Yes!"*

"Well, turn the sonofabitch off," Kevlin commanded.

"I can't." Desperation.

"No way?"

"I'd have done it if I could, shithead. Let me out of here."

"At least nobody else goes when that baby blows."

"Fuck you," Corky snarled. "You're too late."

"Maybe not quite." Kevlin's voice was harsh with emotion and fatigue. He couldn't leave a fellow sailor below. "Time for you to get on deck."

He slipped the lock off the hatch cover, raising his ax in warning. Corky pushed his way into the cockpit. His head was bloody from his fall, his eyes wild and angry, his scar livid.

He jerked himself up and looked over the cockpit at the bow, its tip buried in white water. "You sonofabitch."

"Kiss her goodbye," Kevlin said. "But you're coming with me.

Voluntarily—or not. You've got a lot to answer for to the authorities. Hold out your hands." Corky drew back for a moment.

"Now!" Kevlin brandished the ax, and Corky put his hands together. "Do it my way. It's your only ticket out."

With one hand, Kevlin grabbed a roll of duct tape he had taken from the locker and lashed it around Corky's wrists.

With Corky's hands bound, Kevlin laid down his ax and slid over the side of the cockpit. He winched the line tethering the speedboat forward.

"Get in..." But out of the corner of his eye, he saw Corky move.

*   *   *

Corky slammed a shoulder into him, knocking him overboard. As he fell, he grabbed the stern with one fist, hanging on. The force of the water bounced him about.

"Fuck you, too, you goddam Boy Scout." Corky stood, sneering, and ripped the tape loose with his teeth.

He picked up the ax and held it above his head. There was no question of his intent; Kevlin let go and splashed backward into the water.

The speedboat towed by *Solo Eagle* nearly ran him down. Kevlin dodged to one side, swam desperately to the stern and pulled himself on board.

A furious Corky slammed the ax down on the speedboat's tether, cutting the line.

Solo Eagle flew away.

"See you in hell," Corky yelled.

Corky jumped to the helm and began cursing as he wrestled the wheel, trying to bring the boat around. The steering gear was jammed—the boat could only run downwind.

Kevlin had seen to that with his ax blows.

He screamed something as Kevlin started the powerboat's big engine and gunned the powerboat around.

He jammed the throttle to the firewall. The boat leaped ahead.

Hurry.

Time passed agonizingly. He was entering the big Heads.

How much time did he have left? He stole a glance over his shoulder. Behind him, *Solo Eagle* began to turn.

Kevlin was pursued by death.

He had done it. Somehow he turned the sinking vessel about. Corky raised his fist aloft in a triumphant self-congratulatory gesture. He grinned his lop-sided pirate-like grin at Kevlin.

Then it happened so quickly that Kevlin blinked in disbelief.

*　　*　　*

Her low-riding bow seemed to spear into a wave and the aft section raised like a teeter totter. Her mast tipped sideways, her sails shuddered, and then she began to tip forward in a final plunge to the depths.

In the cockpit, Corky stood maniacally gripping the wheel. He was the skipper; he would drive his boat to hell.

Then the green waters closed over them without a trace: Corky, *American Solo* and its lethal cargo disappeared under the sea, just a few kilometers south and east of the Heads.

Kevlin stared. Maybe, just maybe, in the pressure of the terrible depths, the sailboat's lead keel casing might fracture and break apart. Salt water could destroy the electronics.

And kill that thing.

The deadline? It had passed, Kevlin figured.

He could relax. He found he was perspiring heavily, with his heart pounding.

*　　*　　*

The sky turned blue, with unlimited visibility. Above was a golden technicolor sun. The westerly felt good on Kevlin's perspiring face as he passed the protection of the mighty Sydney Heads—and turned into safe harbor.

"Thank God, it's over," Kevlin reassured himself.

He was reaching his hand forward to throttle back when there was a concussive roar and a searing, blinding flash.

All the world erupted in a mushroom-shaped cloud.

79

THE LIGHT WAS SEARING, a blue-white flash like a million-power strobe. The sky seemed to crack open and the shock wave blasted into the huge Sydney Heads, demolishing everything on the seaward slopes and tearing off huge boulders.

The fireball reached its maximum size one second after the explosion, rearing high in the sky and carrying millions of tons of water. Thermal radiation, hotter than the sun at 9,000 degrees Fahrenheit, spread outward with the speed of light and blistered everything within miles of ground zero, where the bomb had exploded.

Winds at several hundred miles an hour screamed like banshees toward the Sydney Heads, which bore the brunt of the explosion. They burst over the Heads, pushed through the harbor entryway and slammed toward Sydney's bustling inner harbor and glittering Downtown. Stronger than several hurricanes, the winds scoured and tore anything that stood in their path.

Then came the tidal wave.

A wall of water taller than several houses, vertical and foaming, roared through the Heads' entryway. In its devastating fury, trees, houses, beaches, cars, people, and even boulders were swept away. Sea-going boats were buried under tons of water; some flew onto shore like crumpled toys.

The towering wave attacked the city's harbor with a cold rage, slamming into skyscrapers, producing a maelstrom of twisted metal and concrete. All along the waterfront, people ran, screamed and prayed.

Sydney was in chaos.

80

THE WAVE kept growing, higher and higher. He cried out as it overtook his boat, shook it and lifted its stern. His boat jumped skyward, the sea blurring, the wind howling.

He was on an out-of-control escalator, flinging him ever upward. He glimpsed mists of white beneath the towering green.

He gave the wheel a shove to port, hoping to present the boat's stern to the wave, the classic blue water survival technique, but he was lifted helplessly on the wave and twisted about.

The boat cocked at a crazy angle and he plunged downward, engines roaring helplessly, deeper and deeper into the green abyss.

The bow slammed and speared under.

The maelstrom engulfed him. An icy fist of water roared back at Kevlin, smashing the windshield and slugging him.

It tore his grasp from the wheel. The water was cold and unrelenting, churned up from the dark depths. The turbulence was beyond belief.

The boat flipped over.

He blacked out. No pain. No qualms.

Then back again. He shook his head and snapped his eyes upward.

White. A bright light. He felt as if he were on an elevator, rising toward it without effort.

I'm dead, he thought.

*   *   *

He opened his eyes, spitting out seawater. He bobbed violently about; with great effort, he tried to focus his eyes.

He was in the harbor, just inside the protection of the South

Head. He breathed deeply: he was still alive. The explosion had gone off at sea, in the depths, and the Heads had absorbed at least some of the deadly bomb.

With that knowledge came a glimmer of hope. He raised his head up as far out of the water as he could. Pain hit him; his vision swam. What about True—was she still alive? Was Sydney still standing?

In the near distance he saw a beach. Protected by the South Head, which had taken the brunt of the blast, it had escaped much of the wave and most of the explosion. He paddled toward it until he could wade ashore. The warm sands beneath his toes felt good; he had lost his shoes in the accident.

He had to get back.

The beach had been torn up by the rush of the tidal water. All that remained of the private docks were a few pilings, passed up by the surging water. Then he saw it in a tangle of brush and fallen trees: a bright flash of painted metal. A tiny jet ski.

Moving his bruised body painfully, he dragged the tiny watercraft back to the water, then yanked the starter chord.

He listened, but could not hear the engine run—until he leaned on the bicycle-like handlebars and cracked the throttle. The craft leaped forward, its engine snarling—nearly unseating him.

He had lost his hearing.

He roared across the choppy waters toward Downtown Sydney, barely in control of himself. The jet ski churned onward, bobbing frantically, fighting a strong outflow of water. It had to be the outsurge of the tidal wave.

He gasped as he saw what it uncovered. In front of him lay what was left of Sydney Harbor, dark and glistening ominously. Boats had been tossed up on beaches, clawed apart; buildings were windowless, some had collapsed.

The city was in chaos.

He sped past the Opera House, now just a skeleton, her sail-like white roofs in shreds, her glass blown out. From somewhere to the west, helicopters thundered and sirens wailed.

The pier area was a jumble of splintered timbers, broken casements and twisted sheets of steel. The boatyard was covered with dark pools of water and shattered glass. But the main building had survived.

Dangling forlornly by one bracket was the sign, "Great Barrier Reef Boat Yard."

Kevlin hastily beached his jet ski.

There was a roaring in his head but he could make out sounds of water rushing back to the sea. His hearing was coming back.

From inside the boat shop came a banging noise. He raised his head to listen. Someone emerged from the darkened doorway, carrying a shapeless bundle.

A girl. A lovely girl, with long legs and short blonde hair that glistened in the sunlight.

She looked up, dropping her armful, and shading her eyes. They grew wild.

"Oh, God," she exclaimed. She ran to him, her arms outstretched as though she was already holding him.

"You're not dead!"

Tears started, but only framed the incredible smile on her face. "True, I am so glad...."

He was about to say more when a police car splashed into the yard. Someone else had observed his progress through the harbor.

A harried Sydney policeman confronted him.

"We've finally caught up with you! And you've got a lot to answer for."

81

INVESTIGATOR Les Morrehead slammed his way into the interrogation room. He looked harried and rumpled. "What the bloody hell did you do out there?"

The menace was unmistakable.

"We had *Solo Eagle* under surveillance from the air."

"You saw me sailing *away* from the harbor."

"So you knew about the bomb."

"I was trying to save lives."

"More likely, you turned yellow. Couldn't' carry it off."

Kevlin blinked in surprise and sat up straighter. More bruises made themselves known. This was coming out all wrong. "I tried to warn everyone. Remember?"

"If you're so bloody innocent, how'd you know about a bomb in the first place?"

"Something was wrong with the keel."

The inspector leaned forward in his chair. "You and your terrorist pals hatched a plan to blackmail Sydney. But something went wrong. You tried to run for it." A cynical smile crossed his face: "Didn't get very far, did you?"

Kevlin was getting angry. "Okay, rewind this to the beginning. Every racer had secrets, but Bowman and *Eagle* made no attempt to hide. Why?"

"Suppose you tell me."

"He wanted everyone to see the keel. It was odd—oversized. Bowman passed it off at the time as a secret design."

The inspector began to get up. "Doesn't add up."

"I didn't think much about it at the time. The boat had an odd motion. It hobby horsed." Kevlin glared at him. "That meant it rocked back and forth, like a rocking chair. There wasn't enough weight far enough down below. When I was in the hospital, watching the TV ceremonies, I saw that as they ran clips of the boat in the ocean.

"Inside the hollow keel bulb was the bomb—one of the 'suit-case bombs' that the Russians report missing from their nuclear stockpile from time to time, when it suits them. They come in various sizes. The small suitcase nukes are carried in a backpack, but a medium-sized one is about the size of a 50-gallon diesel fuel drum .

"The medium-size nukes weigh 300 to 400 pounds—actually not very heavy ballast for its size, even with its lead casing. Those racing bulb keels can run up to 10,000 pounds. That was what was giving Bowman the problem."

"More likely you and Bowman were a pair. How else would you know about a bomb—unless you were in on it from the beginning?"

"One of the killers told me."

The inspector snorted disdainfully. "

"True Whitman and I tracked him down in *Jolly Swagwoman*." Kevlin continued, "He destroyed Lord Harwood and his craft. He nearly got us."

The inspector looked incredulous.

"Sakko Shuro Maginawa. He'd been sabotaging boats that had a certain kind of ballast: depleted uranium. That included Marci Whitman's racer.

"He...he killed our Marci?"

"Rigged her boat with an incendiary device. It burned off a structural part of the carbon fiber keel so that at the height of the storm, the keel tore off with the ballast bulb and the boat cap-sized. Flipped over. With her under it. No question: She was mur-dered."

"He actually admitted to you he killed Marci?"

"He flatly said he got them all—all the boats with the spent uranium ballast.

"Why?"

"He was an agent of some sort— a fanatical counter terrorist. In his dying moments, he told me the bomb was on one of the boats with the spent uranium keel."

"So this Sakko killed them all?"

"Before he died, he boasted he didn't know which boat carried the bomb—so he took no chances. He said something like, "What's a few lives compared to millions? Just numbers."

"Why didn't he get Bowman?"

"He wasn't sure. First, he went after boats with known depleted uranium keels. Bowman's was reputed to be made of lead. At the end, he must have been on to something. He kept saying, *Sid.* That was all he could get out as a warning. I finally figured out Sid was short for Sydney.

"Why didn't you turn the bloody bomb off?"

"Couldn't. It was on a double-down timer. If I tried to disconnect it, that would have set off a backup switch. Boom."

"So you decided to sail away."

"Yeah. I got out past the Heads and took a sharp turn to starboard. I could see I didn't have a lot of time left. The boat was damaged and sank deep in the Tasman Sea. I barely got off in time. The sea must have taken the brunt of the underwater explosion—and the Heads deflected a lot of the blast. Mostly, what Sydney got was the winds over the Heads and the waves through the entryway. The result was bad, but nowhere near what would have happened if it had gone off at Ground Zero—Downtown Sydney's harbor."

"And Bowman?"

"He tried to stop me—and went down with his boat." Kevlin paused, his brow furrowed in thought. "What are you charging me with."

The inspector arose, his face impassive. "We'll have to work on that, won't we?" he said.

" In your case, there are so many lovely options we don't know which ones we'll finally go with. But in the meantime, you've found a home."

SECTION
FIVE

THE
LONG
VOYAGE
HOME

8 2

THE SMALL SAILBOAT drifted through the foggy San Diego harbor and bumped lightly against the large white hull.

Kevlin stole a quick glance up the shadowy gangway. No one was there to meet him, but then again, he didn't expect a welcoming committee.

They had heard him arrive? Someone would be inside.

Waiting.

He tied his craft alongside *Corinthian II* and painfully clambered up the metal stairs. His leg throbbed painfully and his hands still hurt.

He might as well get this over with: He doubted if he even had a job left.

*   *   *

Inside, there was a whir of air conditioning and the temperature dropped at least 20 degrees.

She was seated behind her massive desk, one hand in a desk drawer, her watchful face a tight mask. Not blinking.

"Welcome back, Kevlin," she said. He was listening carefully. There was no welcome in her voice.

"Thanks," he said, involuntarily turning away. He scratched his nose.

"Reporting in? After all this time? One wonders why you bother." Her eyes were black marbles.

"Sam, we've got to work this out. I got all tangled up in the story, and, for a while the Aussie cops even thought that I was involved. In the bomb."

"You convinced them otherwise?"

"Yeah. They figured it out."

"Really?" She took her time.

"But I've got an inside story about the race and its secrets. The murders. And a first-person account of the final moments onboard the racer with the bomb that went off and demolished Sydney's harbor."

"Most of it's already been all over TV and the papers."

She carefully lit a cigarette. Waiting.

He took a deep breath. "Here's something. I'm closing in on the killers."

"Are you, now?" Sam puffed on her cigarette. "Have you got something to go on? I mean, *real* facts?"

He had the feeling she was toying with him.

"I was on the *Satari* when it was sinking. Sakko boasted he had an accomplice. Someone he said that I knew and trusted."

"Sakko told you that? You're sure?" She leaned forward, now very interested.

"Before he died, he talked. Boasted actually."

"Did he say?"

"No. But as he talked, there was a voice on his radio. He was tuned in to someone. I couldn't make out the words. But the voice was...a familiar one."

He waited a moment.

"You know how crazy that all sounds?" Sam leaned forward in an easy motion, her eyes growing cold. She raised her arm from beneath her desk.

In her hand was a tiny, black automatic pistol.

83

S HE RAISED THE GUN CASUALLY, aiming it directly at his chest. Her face hardened into a murderous mask.

His eyes were drawn to Sam's tiny pistol, waving back and forth at him. It was an easily hidden gun with a very small caliber bullet. An assassin's short-range pistol.

Deadly, in the right hands.

He had totally underestimated her. Looking into her glittering eyes he saw the consequences—his own death.

Her finger toyed with the trigger. "Kevlin. I wish I could say it's been grand. But you've been a pain in the ass from day one."

"Thanks." He tried a desperate ploy. "Why'd you do it?"

She ignored him, thought for a moment, and pressed a dial on her cell phone."If you've got everything ready," she said almost casually, "Come down now."

Then it came to him:

Something about her voice. When she talked on the telephone, it was lower, broader—a telephone voice.

That one. He'd heard it before.

"It was you! You were the voice on the Sakko's radio. On the *Satari.* You were giving him orders."

"You're finally catching up."

Her eyes glowed. She surveyed Kevlin in the chair and picked up a cigarette and lit it.

"We've got a few moments to kill. Pardon the expression. It wasn't Sakko's fault that Australian bitch was out in a storm. He wasn't ordered to kill Marci. Just drop her keel.

"She's dead just the same. And the others?"

"The crazy Frenchman killed himself. You know how their racers are. The way we figure it, he was way overcanvassed in that storm, caught a wave wrong and capsized."

"We....?"

"The New Zealander lost his boat in the ice fields...but survived. Wasn't it a hoot that Corky rescued him?"

She managed a mirthless laugh.

"And Lord Harwood?"

"Damn thing wouldn't go off. The bomb must've fizzled. Sakko had to take care of business....the old fashioned way."

"I was there. The bastard."

She exhaled a large cloud of cigarette smoke toward him. "Listen, Kevlin: For the record, not that it matters much right now, Sakko wasn't the bad guy. He was trying to destroy the bomb. "

"But he didn't know which racer had the bomb."

She paused for a moment as she licked her lips. "Sakko went after all the boats that were suspect."

"All those sailors..dead. My God!"

"What's a few lives when you are trying to save millions of people?" She shrugged."Just numbers."

"Who are they."

"Wealthy financiers."

"I'm not buying that."

"You're not in a position to buy much of anything. Actually, it's none of your fucking business."

"Tell me this: Who was behind Corky—and the bomb?"

"Ah, we come to that." She glanced at the office clock and smiled. "Did you ever wonder how Corky Bowman entered that multi-million dollar race on tattered jeans and six-pack money? Or how he finally got his 'lead' keel?"

"I'm catching up."

"Behind Corky was GAAFF: the Great American Alpha First Federation. It's an ultra right-wing hate group. It hates foreigners. Hates imports. Hates the loss of jobs. Especially hates the power growing in the Pacific Rim.

"Enter the bomb?"

"If you're a small group, nothing makes a statement like a bomb. Every hate group knows that. Here's the cute part. Their plan was to blame the Pacific Rim conglomerate."

When Kevlin frowned, she added. "It's easy enough. All you have to do is send an E-mail. A recorded message to a radio station; maybe a tape with a hooded spokesperson to TV. Put it on the YouTube. A couple of the social networks. A well-pieced together bit of fiction to claim the attack as a Pacific Rim victory."

"So?"

"You've got to be joking. The world would turn against them. The Pacific Rim would lose billions. Billions."

"It couldn't be proven."

She grinned mirthlessly."Wouldn't need to be. That's the beauty of it. The Pacific Rim corporations would spend millions denying a charge they were innocent of and still end up losing their asses in the long run."

"With no evidence."

"No one would do business with them. Customers would shun them. The public relations nightmare would eat them alive, no matter what the courts decided. They were screwed, any which way they turned."

"Uh, the bomb went off..."

"Yeah, and thanks to you, it was botched beyond belief. Everyone saw you racing through the harbor on TV. Trying to save Sydney. Making it blow up out in the Tasman Sea. My magazine editor. It was obvious where the bomb was aboard that boat, and an investigation might point back to who put it there in the first place. So I suppose the conglomerate will lay low...for a while. And wait until this blows over."

*   *   *

Kevlin felt shaky. Red spots danced in front of his eyes. He felt like falling out of his chair.

"Why did this have to happen in Sydney?"

She brightened. "Terrific target. Great opportunity. Sydney is an international mecca. Look back: there's one city every decade that's the place to be. The city that glitters. In the 1920s, it was

Paris. In the 60s, it was London; in the 70s, New York. Now, it's Sydney...er...was Sydney."

"What the hell did the bomb have to do with the race?"

Sam took a deep puff on the cigarette. "It's not easy transporting an explosive device, especially a sophisticated nuclear one. They're on the lookout, you know. But sailboat keels are below water. Way below."

She managed a wan smile. "Here's the beauty part. With keels ballasted with depleted plutonium, a plutonium bomb is undetectable."

She stubbed out the cigarette. "We've nattered away enough, Kevlin."

She waved the pistol lazily at him: "You see, you're history. You're all done. You'll resign from the magazine and take off on that long South Seas cruise you've always talked about onboard your *Leaky Teaky.*"

"Ah, God." Kevlin looked hard at her, sensing what was coming.

"One switch." She pointed the black automatic unwaveringly at his heart. "You'll head out to sea—and in the grand tradition of seafarers—never be heard from again. Happy now?"

Now he knew.

There was a knock on the door.

"It's about time," said Sam.

The blow to the back of his head hurt Kevlin and the last thing he remembered was that he toppled forward and cracked his head against the desk.

Then it all went black.

84

B EAR was at the helm of Kevlin's sailboat, his massive fists gripping the tiller. The engine was humming busily—Bear was not a sailing man and obviously preferred the diesel.

Kevlin lay shivering in the grating of the teak cockpit. His hands and his ankles were bound with duct tape. He was slowly awakening. His head hurt.

"Sorry 'bout that," said the Bear, looking down apologetically. "We'll try to get this over with pronto."

The roll of the boat told him that they had passed Point Loma and were now in the Pacific. Heading offshore.

"Don't hurry on my account," Kevlin said, between clenched teeth. "How far we going tonight, Mr. Bear?"

"Not far, old buddy. And lay off that *Mr.* business."

"Been wondering about things. Can you talk?"

Bear looked down, amused. "If you're not going anywhere. It'll help pass the time."

*　　*　　*

"How'd Sam get involved in all this?"

"Not the smartest thing she's gotten into." Bear shook his head.

"Let me take a shot at this. Sam lives awfully high. The big boat and all. She got into deep financial trouble. Am I on track?"

"Sounds about right. Yeah, she needed money, all right. Lots of money."

"Don't tell me she got into this just for the bloody dollars."

"She's got a kid. In the Far East now, under special care."

Kevlin suddenly realized how close Sam and Bear were. He was always on board, even when Kevlin left.

Bear smiled wanly. "Mah bunkie. We've been together now for years. I thought you'd tumbled on to it by now."

"Surprises the hell out of me, Bear. But how'd you get into this mess?"

Bear turned away. "Bit by bit, I guess. At the start, Sam's friends came to me with electronic gear. Cutting edge stuff I hadn't even heard of before. Unbelievable stuff. Would I try this out? How about that? They manufacture it, you know. I got whatever I needed, at any time I needed it, plus generous money for "testing." All under the table. A slice of techno-heaven."

"You got into it for the toys?"

"That was the start. Sam said it was OK. Then she came to me to say they had a problem. Heard that some nut was going to blow up a bomb somewhere. Kill lots of innocent people. They wanted to stop it. Would I help? The answer was: sure. For Sam.

"Did you know how they were going to stop the bomb?"

"No idea, at first. They told me that they'd heard that a bomb was rigged to go off in San Diego harbor. Seattle. Or LA. Then maybe New York. or Boston. Somewhere along the route—who knew? At the end I was in too deep. I couldn't go back."

"You tried to get out? Blackmail?"

Bear hung his head. "Don't even ask."

"Sam, too?"

"That kid of hers? They know where Sam keeps her. Do you know what these people are capable of?"

"I've got a good idea. Why'd the conglomerate go after Sam in the first place?"

"Old story. Another billionaire outfit buys another media. With Sam and her magazine in their pocket, they figured they could get instant access to most everything they didn't know before. Not true, of course, but that was their thinking. And they would also get favorable stuff written about them. They'd gain people and money for their cause.

He paused. "No matter what happened: The magazine would be on their side. One way or another."

"For a price. An awful price."

"Old buddy, I am sorry you got so inquisitive about everything. I tried to keep you..."

He was interrupted by the sound of a voice coming from his hand-held VHF radio. "*Teaky*...you there?"

"Yo. Affirmative," Bear responded. He glanced at the GPS indicator and rattled off coordinates.

"See you in five. Out."

*   *   *

"Show's about over," Bear said, apologetically. He flicked on the masthead running lights. "At least you go out like a sailor. It's the best I can do."

Bear put the helm on automatic pilot and ducked below. Kevlin could hear him hammering in the bilge areas. He emerged holding two bronze fittings.

"Your seacocks," Bear announced. He threw them down.

Kevlin swallowed hard. That meant his boat was flooding. Sinking.

"You go down in the best tradition. With your ship." Bear grabbed Kevlin by the feet and, with surprising gentleness, dragged him from the cockpit to the cabin below.

Bear added, "Everybody knows the *Teaky* was taking on water. Needed repair of the old garboards and planking. In fact, I told them."

Kevlin stole a glance below. Water was already rising from the floorboards.

"I won't ask you to get wet...right away." Bear gently placed his friend on the starboard bunk.

"Comfy, for now?"

"Yeah, thanks, Bear." The sarcasm missed.

Bear hung his head for a moment, his eyes misting over. "That's it, then. Sorry, old buddy." He moved through the hatch, and slammed it shut.

Kevlin could hear the snick of the hatch bolt going into place. He was locked below in a sinking boat.

Slowly, in the dark, the water began to rise.

85

THE DISTANT *thump thump* of helicopter blades penetrated the cabin, where Kevlin lay.

Someone was flying in by chopper. *Perfect,* he thought. Bear would get off and be back on land before the boat hit bottom.

There was a crackle of static. *"Teaky....*I have you in sight."

"Yo," Bear said from the cockpit, a moment later. His voice came in clearly through the vents. "All set down here."

Kevlin thrashed angrily in his bunk and fell into the water below. It was inches deep and cold. And rising.

Panting, he slithered forward, dropped to his knees and plunged his hands below the water, grappling with a lid. Inside the tool box he found what he was looking for: a wood chisel. Several bloody minutes later, its razor-sharp tip had cut through his wrist tape.

"Coming alongside," announced the radio voice.

"Come ahead," Bear answered. "Project's all wrapped up here."

Bracing his hands on the cabin wall, Kevlin stole a glance out the porthole.

In the darkness, the yacht's two-man helicopter, its lights flashing, drifted over to hover alongside. Its thunder and down-draft rocked the tiny boat.

At the controls was a small, dark figure, her face illuminated by the dashboard lights. Eyes glittering. Sam.

The helicopter's landing lights flashed on. From below its belly, shining in the light, reeled a stainless steel cable. At the end was a heavy harness.

"Hurry up. Make your move."

"Good to see you, too, sweetie," amiably said Bear.

*   *   *

Kevlin felt around underwater to the place where the water gushed. The seacocks were gone. But there something else was, in the darkness—Bear had missed it.

What every good sailor keeps: plugs of soft, tapered wood for emergencies. He tore one plug off its mounting and jammed it into the hole, stemming the rising tide. He slammed it hard with the ball of his hand.

He did the same for the other missing seacock.

His boat would be safe, momentarily.

The aft hatch was bolted. No way out there, thanks to Bear. But the forward hatch...the forward hatch...latched only from inside.

He splashed forward.

*   *   *

Off to his port side, the helicopter hovered close by. Atop the transom, Bear was balancing his bulk delicately, trying to snag the swinging harness.

"We haven't got all day," Sam barked over the radio. She eased the helicopter closer.

Kevlin carefully opened the forward hatch a few inches. He saw Bear shake his head and smile wanly, tensing his body on his toes. Even in duress, he was trying to please her.

The harness jerked nearer; Bear reached up, delicately balancing his bulk. The boat lurched in the swell, the stern heaved and the end of the line danced just out of reach.

Bear snatched vainly at the air, nearly falling overboard.

Now. Kevlin said a little prayer and launched himself from the hatch, hurtling across the deck to the cockpit.

"Behind you..." came Sam's warning.

"What...?" Bear partly turned, still trying to steady himself.

Kevlin lowered his head and put all his weight into a desperate lunge.

Bear grunted as the blow jarred him sideways. His massive

bulk flew off the end of the transom, splashing heavily into the wake.

Kevlin took a long step forward, judging his timing. It was all or nothing now.

As the dangling cable swung toward him, he made a desperate grab.

Now! Adrenalin pumping, he lunged forward.

His fingers pawed the air for a moment and closed. He held on with all the energy he could muster. In a desperate motion, he threw himself backward into the cockpit and wrapped the cable around a strong cleat. He prayed it wouldn't tear loose under the strain.

"You fucking idiot!" the radio squawked. She was not pleased. "That's not going to do you any good."

"Try me," Kevlin yelled back. *One and done.*

*   *   *

He slammed the engine's throttle forward and the boat's powerful diesel roared. The hull shuddered and began to move, a white plume at its stern.

The sailboat began its deadly tug of war.

A thousand horsepower roared as the helicopter attempted to rise. The steel strands linking them tightened and strained taut.

Kevlin glanced upward, shielding his eyes from the downblast. Sam's face was a mask of murderous fury as she worked the throttle and controls, trying to escape. The noise was horrific.

Kevlin picked up the radio. "Give it up, Sam. It's over."

She raised her left hand and gave him the finger.

The helicopter banked away, cable groaning. The pressure slewed the boat around, waves breaking over the cockpit.

Kevlin threw over the tiller, presenting the sailboat's stern to the chopper; the propeller dug in hard.

With a thump, the thin steel line straightened out.

"You're hooked!" Kevlin yelled, victoriously. "I've got you."

"No, I've got you!" Sam screamed, gunning the helicopter to full power. Instead of rising, the chopper menacingly lowered its nose— barely skimming above the water.

Howling and rattling, it crept nearer.

*   *   *

Kevlin helplessly watched her come.

Alone in the cockpit, he was exposed and without protection.

The noise was horrific; the downdraft ripped at his clothing; spume slammed into his eyes.

He couldn't get away; neither could she. No place to run, no place to hide. There would be only one victor.

The blades churned within inches of his face. Each rotor screamed as it split the air like a giant scimitar.

My God! Kevlin rammed the tiller to starboard. The sailboat dug its shoulder in, slewed about, and yawed wildly to port.

The thick mast swung straight into the roaring blades.

A look of horror came over Sam's face. She had time to scream and yank desperately at the controls.

The carbon fiber blades shattered on impact, splintered dark shards flew everywhere. Their fragments sprayed about like deadly shrapnel, slamming into the boat and rained deadly hail on the water.

For a half second, the chopper hung frozen in mid-air, its engine screaming. Then with a roar, it dropped nose first into the sea.

It struck the crest of a wave, bounced crazily sideways, and skated across the surface.

The broken stubs of the rotors flailed helplessly at the water, twisting it about. From somewhere, there was a loud crack as the impact broke the canopy.

When it came to rest, it lay suspended in the water like a dead thing. Smoke wisped around the cockpit and the pilot.

Sam raised her head once, a pool of blood staining her face. She glared unblinkingly around, her mouth distorted in rage and hate. She looked across the waves and saw Kevlin.

She managed to scream at him once.

The helicopter rolled a final time as its compartments flooded.

It disappeared beneath the waves, leaving behind only an oily slick.

Kevlin stood transfixed, his chest heaving. The adrenalin was wearing off.

*   *   *

Whap. There was a splintering noise as the cable grew taut, grinding into the boat.

Water rushed in the cockpit drain holes as the boat tilted. The helicopter was sinking quickly, dragging the boat under with it.

There was only once chance—a desperate measure.

He yanked the throttle back and spun the boat's stern toward the cable. He'd have to do this right, or end up with cable wrapped around his prop.

Like a buzz saw, the bronze propeller blades screamed. They howled and throbbed as Kevlin pressured them against the bar-taut cable.

The stern popped up out of the water. A short length of cable , its frayed end showing, dangled harmlessly from the transom.

In the sudden silence, Kevlin could feel the blood pounding in his ears. They were free.

"Sam!" he called out, circling back. Despite all she was guilty of, he couldn't leave another human alone to the mercy of the ocean.

He scanned the water, but nothing bobbed to the surface, except a few loose items from the chopper. A floatation pad. A bit of plastic.

The waves marched endlessly, ruthlessly onward.

Gone forever was the architect of the killings and the corrupter of his friend.

*   *   *

Bear was treading water. In the moonlight, his face seemed strangely white

"I'm coming alongside," Kevlin yelled, throttling back.

The engine subsided into a soft growl. Something thumped against the hull as the boat overran debris in the water.

"Get ready to come aboard."

Bear shook his massive head. "No."

The distress of his former friend touched Kevlin. "I can't leave you. We'll find a way out of this mess. You're not in that deep."

"Yeah, I am. I really am." It was a mournful voice. "I heard an explosion. Was that Sam? Is she...?"

"Sam's...gone."

Bear treaded water more slowly, shoving himself away. *"Gone?"*

Kevlin could see blood staining the water.

"Let her go," Kevlin said, shakily. "Let's get you out of here."

A moment of hesitation. "No."

"For old times' sake." Kevlin knelt over the side of the transom, reaching out. "Take my hand."

"Wherever she is, she needs me."

"Where she is, she doesn't need you."

The big hand floated limply, inches away from Kevlin's fingers.

"She does, Kev. She really does...I can feel it."

He stopped treading water.

"Come on!" Kevlin cried out. He strained to close the gap.

Bear reached out and gently brushed Kevlin's hand away.

"See you around, old buddy," said Bear, slowly exhaling.

It was as if a great weight had been lifted from him. He had made his decision; his face became peaceful and serene.

With a quick motion of his arms, he slipped beneath the surface.

The water reached up to enclose him.

For only a moment, there was a silvery trail on the surface.

And then the bubbles stopped.

EPILOGUE

86

A SPECTRAL MOON illuminated the dark waters of San Diego harbor. Warm breezes flowed past Point Loma from the nearby ocean toward the small wooden sailboat, tugging playfully at its anchor.

Kevlin had made his decision: he'd head westward for the Hawaiian Islands, and, from there cruise into the deep reaches of the South Pacific. He wanted to be away from land. Away from people.

Get lost for a while.

He would be alone on the longest voyage of his life, wandering through the Pacific islands. In the process, he would have time to heal himself. Physically and mentally.

He could handle his own sailboat. Solo. In the grand tradition of mariners. No crew, no problems.

*   *   *

What had happened to *Megasail's* owner and its communication's officer?

The police had interviewed him about the disappearance, but after a few rounds of intensive interviews and taped statements, they seemed to have lost interest. Kevlin didn't really seem to know. Maybe Sam and Bear took off in the chopper to look at some boats and simply never returned.

Another mystery of the sea. It happened all the time in the old port city of San Diego. An accident. Unexplained.

If an extended inquiry should come up, he'd have to be interviewed further. But they'd have to find him first.

And the South Pacific was a big place. Real big.

He had spent some time carefully outfitting his sailboat with gear and provisions for a long voyage. He had *Leaky Teaky* pulled out of the water at a San Diego boatyard that understood wooden hulls and had the garboard planks replaced.

He'd worked on them himself along with the yard workers. Then he'd recaulked the hull and repainted it. Everything was in readiness.

Now he and his boat were ready for a long, long voyage.

He didn't have a lot of money left but where he was going he didn't need much. He had back salary credited to his account in a local bank. Also, he had written a follow-up *Megasail* article, *Trapped Upside Down,* and entered it in the BWI writing awards contest (Seamanship and Survival category). That story about his entrapment under the overturned racer *Jolly Swagwoman* and his days of survival inside the hull had proved to be good for a First Place award and cash money.

An odd thought came to him. Sam would have been proud, sort of. He had come through and that was why he had been hired: to win some awards.

*   *   *

In another part of the world, the Race Alone Around the World was continuing in the Atlantic, off the coast of Brazil. The Australian sailor who had replaced Marci was in the lead.

They were now in their final lap back to New York.

There were no more incidents. Or accidents.

But for Kevlin, the race was over. He had resigned from the magazine. It didn't matter.

He knew where he was headed: Australia.

Sydney was rebuilding itself. The outer harbor was in shambles, but the spirit of the great city was manifesting itself. It was a land of comebacks. This would be just one more.

Somewhere at the end of the voyage, he knew, True would be waiting for him. There'd be a new life for him down under when he got there.

He had a boat and the ancient stars to help guide him. A vast ocean of wonder and healing lay ahead of him. He wondered why he felt so hollow, drained of feelings and cold inside.

This was the beginning of the voyage he had dreamed about.

*　　*　　*

He looked up for a moment to savor the moon's unusual brightness. There were fingers of ghostly mist playing around its edges.

It was all so promising, as if something were in the atmosphere.

The sea breeze seemed to stir in the night air, redolent of flowers. The scents reminded him of Marci.

A wave of nostalgia swept over him. He missed her so much. He felt his eyes misting over.

Enough. It was time to get underway.

There was a light splash near the bow.

He lifted his head. *Something.*

Mists had rolled in from the sea, draping the bow in a luminous whiteness.

Odd.

He glanced away for a moment toward shore, where the lights of thousands of homes twinkled. It'd be the last he'd see of civilization for a long time and it made him feel lonely.

If only...

Something—again on the bow.

A peculiar feeling sent chills up his spine.

The mist was gone.

*　　*　　*

She stood in silhouette, illuminated by the ghostly moonlight, her short blonde hair ruffling in the light breeze.

She wore white shorts and blouse as she had when he first met her so long ago. She seemed to levitate on the deck as she came closer.

Emotions clutched at his throat and his heart pounded. His eyes began to blur. It could not be.

"Is it you?"

She did not answer for a moment, but just smiled that wide, beautiful smile. She moved a wisp of blonde hair from her forehead. Her blue eyes were warm and direct.

He stepped forward, dizzy with hope.

A thousand times he had dreamt of being with her again, aching to touch her, to hold her.

He reached out with shaking hands, but she gently glided away out of his reach.

With a jolt, he understood that he would never again feel her body, her touch or the passion of her kiss. In that instant, he began to understand.

By going on his voyage, he reconnected with her and their eternal love.

The moon. The stars. The ocean.

Somehow she was there. For him.

"You won't be alone," she seemed to promise.

"Come with me?" he pleaded. "Stay?"

"Look at me."

He gazed long and well and a sense of well being flowed into him. A sweet kind of harmony; something truly special. It was a trance from which he wished never to awaken.

And an understanding. He had his love beside him.

He would never be alone again.

*   *   *

Some time later, a small boat sailed quietly out of the harbor, moving in the dark waters, the cockpit open to the stars.

A lone sailor was at the helm, resplendent in the moonlight.

And by his side, something beautiful shimmered.

ACKNOWLEDGEMENTS

THE GUY I was seated next to was very quiet, in fact, too quiet. He sat upright in his chair, kind of tense, his head straightforward, his arms crossed. He had a deep sailor's tan, and he was a thin, wiry guy who was intent on the movie we were both seeing about his adventures in the Vendee Globe Race, which he won in his class.

Mike Plant was an unlikely looking racer in a most unusual race for sailors. All he had done, and intended to do once again, was sail alone in a huge boat blasting around the world nonstop. He'd not only be circumnavigating, but he also would be racing other sailors through storms, huge seas, giant waves and even icebergs.

We had talked about doing a book about his adventures.

But when he attempted to sail his giant sailboat, *Coyote*, across the North Atlantic in its first ocean crossing in an attempt to qualify by sailing 2,000 miles alone, he mysteriously went missing. Mike was never found, though his 60-foot Open Class sloop was finally located, floating upside down. It was missing part of its keel.

I was a member of the Mike Plant committee, headed by Capt. Thom Burns, and I recall talking on the phone to the Minnesota governor's office and reporting that French frogmen had gone under the overturned hull and looked about. They did not find Mike and the life raft was still there. "There were no other possibilities," I said.

Mike was missing at sea, permanently.

I wrote about the final voyage of *Coyote* in my book, *Broken Seas*, and the mysterious disappearance of Mike Plant stayed with me. All of us in the sailing world were feeling remorse and a profound sense of loss. What had happened out there?

Dead on the Wind was inspired by Mike and other solo sailors' raw courage and tenacity against what seemed like all odds against the ancient enemy, the sea. This true life story morphed into fiction and the mystery of death at sea took on a new form.

What I learned from solo sailors came alive in my mind in a dramatic new way. In this novel, I speculate on many aspects of at-sea adventures, triumphs and tragedies—and rare, magnificent accomplishments.

I have invented others–including a whole new boating race (Race Alone Around the World—the RAAW) and set it in the time period that many consider to have been the Golden Age of Solo sailing, the 1990s, when everything seemed possible and that terrible things never happened, until, of course they finally did.

It's important to note that there is a vast difference between writing the nonfiction books I have done and this, my first work of fiction. In fiction, the author controls time and commands events. Plot is everything. The nautical things you write about have to be plausible in the reader's mind and ring true in the expert's experience.

But above all, the book of fiction is a work for the reader's mind. His or her imagination must soar with the turning of pages and enter a dimension of the mind. That's fiction at its best.

I want to thank some folks for bearing up during the imagineering and writing of this maritime techno-thriller and mystery. My late wife, Loris, was kind during the long periods of my hand wringing, biting oneself in the back, and the awful "what ifs" that every novelist goes through. My son, Will, helped grandly with plot details and to my surprise, turned out to be a splendid plotter, and I wish him well in his own fiction books.

I would especially thank Kathy Roach, of beautiful San Diego, a noted ocean racer herself, for her feedback and commentary. John Harris, of North Oaks, Minnesota, gave me encouragement and a retired international lawyer's viewpoint. From Annapolis noted naval designer Rodger Martin sent along sailing polars from his beautiful design, *Coyote*, and Herb McCormick, senior editor for *Cruising World,* let me draw on his extensive experience about large racing sailboats. He had sailed aboard racing Open Class boats, including *Coyote.*

Dudley Dix wrote about his adventures in a boisterous Cape-to-Rio ocean race in which the rudder broke on his own 36-foot sloop, *Black Cat.* I am grateful to this naval architect for sharing details of how he steered his boat back through high seas and winds by the innovative use of a bucket. This experience, which he wrote about in *Professional BoatBuilder* and later on, in *Cruising World,* forms the basis of the at-sea boat rescue performed by Kevlin aboard *Kiwi* when the racer's rudders break and the hero of this novel uses a bucket attached to ropes as a sort of drogue to steer the boat. It was no ordinary bucket, Dudley assured me, but a South African construction bucket. Very sturdy.

My thanks also to friends, Barb and Jul Nickerson, who were taking out their trawler on Puget Sound when they noticed that the water level had risen alarmingly in the bilge. They made it back to harbor, and while Captain Jul worked on his diesel engine, Barb read a PDF of this book on her smart phone. She texted back messages to me. Later, when we had lunch together, Captain Jul gave me some more important feedback especially from his days aboard an icebreaker in the Roaring Forties, Howling Fifties, and Screaming Sixties. I also did not know an icebreaker could break a prop, but he was witness to one such situation.

From California came more suggestions and idea from an old U.S. Armored Infantry buddy of mine, Dennis Renault. Dennis is another sailor with a lot of experience in small boats.

I am especially indebted to the help from Gerard Salmon, from Australia. Ged is an old acquaintance of mine on the Internet and he sails a 16-foot Hartley sloop in Australia's Great Barrier Reef area, usually alone. Ged pointed out to me that extraordinary wave action along the Australian East Coast is not infrequent in geological terms. He tells me that in Aboriginal mythology there is a legend called the Great White Wave. He says that geologists were able to scientifically establish that there was a giant wave that swept over the Heads and hit the Sydney area about 500 years ago. It was the day, according to Aboriginal legends, that "the ocean fell out of the sky." Another report told of how Tasmania had one of Australia's biggest recorded waves at 18.4 meters high. The same storm brought waves three meters or more high into Sydney.

The Vendee Globe, a single-handed nonstop race around the world, again will run in 2016. It is ocean racing at its best and most dangerous. It is the world's toughest ocean race, the "Everest of the sea," that begins with solo sailors leaving Les Sables-d'Olone, France, shooting down the Atlantic Ocean along the old clipper ship route and circumnavigating during the astral summer in the Southern Ocean. The racing is spectacular in wild sailing conditions as racers transmit images via satellite link-ups. (Check out the Vendee Globe race on your Internet search engine and pull up some of the images of the racers in storm conditions.) The Vendee's Open 60-class boats are remarkably similar to the fictional racers of *Dead on the Wind*. I cannot help but wonder how my old sailing friend, Mike Plant, would have done if he were still alive and competing. The Vendee is the around-the-world race for solo sailors that *Dead on the Wind's* race is loosely based upon.

My special thanks to designer Theresa Gedig, whose inspiration resulted in this novel's splendid cover. Theresa came up with the final cover design which had darkness top and bottom, mirroring the cover title, but then that wonderful and inspiration slash of golden light in the center, where that little sailboat voyages off into the horizon. I love it.

Lastly, though many people have been kind enough to look over this novel, I alone am responsible for any errors, omissions or oversights. I thank them for their help, but when I sail, I sail alone.

So it is with novel writing.

—Marlin Bree

The author welcomes readers' thoughts and questions. His website is *www.marlin-bree.com.* and his e-mail is *marlin.marlor@minn.net*

Marlin Bree is a nationally recognized marine journalist who has written extensively about solo sailing adventures. A former magazine editor for the *Minneapolis Tribune,* Bree is a two-time winner of Boating Writers International's prestigious Grand Prize Writing Award. He is the author of numerous boating books including *Wake of the Green Storm, In the Teeth of the Northeaster, Broken Seas: True Tales of Extraordinary seafaring Adventures,* as well as *the Boat Log & Record.* He has done most of his own solo sailing in a 20-foot epoxy-wood boat, *Persistence* (pictured above) that he built himself over a seven-year period beside his home in Shoreview, MN. His website, with photos of the boat and more info on the author, is *www.marlinbree.com.*